"Sharp and funny throughout, [Babitz] offers an almost cinematic portrait of Los Angeles: gritty, glamorous, toxic and intoxicating."

—*The New York Times*

"*Eve's Hollywood* has become a classic of L.A. life. The names in the dedication, Jim Morrison, David Geffen, Andy Warhol, Stephen Stills, and more, indicate the era and depth of this important book."

—Steve Martin

"Eve Babitz is to prose what Chet Baker, with his light, airy style, lyrical but also rhythmic, detached but also sensuous, is to jazz, or what Larry Bell, with his glass confections, the lines so clean and fresh and buoyant, is to sculpture. She's a natural. Or gives every appearance of being one, her writing elevated yet slangy, bright, bouncy, cheerfully hedonistic—L.A. in its purest, most idealized form."

—Lili Anolik, *Vanity Fair*

"Eve Babitz is a little like Madame de Sevigne, that inveterate letter-writer of Louis XIV's time, transposed to the Chateau Marmont in the late 20th-Century—lunching, chatting, dressing, loving and crying in Hollywood, that latter-day Versailles."

—Mollie Gregory, *Los Angeles Times*

"*Eve's Hollywood* is less a straightforward story or tell-all than a sure-footed collection of elliptical yet incisive vignettes and essays about love, longing, beauty, sex, friendship, art, artifice, and above all, Los Angeles . . . Reading West (and Fante and Chandler and Cain and the like) made me want to go to Los Angeles. Babitz makes me feel like I'm there."

—Deborah Shapiro, *The Second Pass*

"Her writing took multiple forms, from romans à clef to essayistic cultural commentaries to reviews to urban-life vignettes to short stories. But in the center was always Babitz and her sensibility—fun and hot and smart, a Henry James–loving party girl . . . The joy of Babitz's writing is in her ability to suggest that an experience is very nearly out of language while still articulating its force within it."

—*New Republic*

"What truly sets Babitz apart from L.A. writers like Didion or Nathanael West . . . is that no matter what cruel realities she might face, a part of her still buys the Hollywood fantasy, feels its magnetic pull as much as that Midwestern hopeful who heads to the coast in pursuit of 'movie dreams.'"

—Steffie Nelson, *Los Angeles Review of Books*

"As the cynosure of the counterculture, Eve Babitz knew everybody worth knowing; slept with everybody worth sleeping with and better still, made herself felt in every encounter."

—Daniel Bernardi, *PopMatters*

"Her dishy, evocative style has never been characterized as Joan Didion–deep but it's inarguably more fun and inviting, providing equally sharp insights on the mood and meaning of Southern California."

—Laura Pearson, *Chicago Tribune*

"Undeniably the work of a native, in love with her place. This quality of the intrinsic and the indigenous is precisely what has been missing from almost all the fiction about Hollywood . . . The accuracy and feeling with which she delineates LA is a fresh quality in California writing."

—Larry McMurtry, *The Washington Post*

"In these ten cajoling tales, Los Angeles is the patient, the heroine, hero, victim, and aggressor: the tales a marvel of free-form madness. Like Renata Adler, Eve Babitz has fact, never telling too much."

—*Vogue*

Sex & Rage

ADVICE to
YOUNG LADIES
EAGER for
a GOOD TIME.

a novel by

Eve Babitz

COUNTERPOINT
BERKELEY, CALIFORNIA

First Counterpoint paperback edition: July 2017

Library of Congress Cataloging-in-Publication Data
Names: Babitz, Eve, author.
Title: Sex and rage : advice to young ladies eager for a good time / Eve
    Babitz.
Description: Counterpoint Edition. | Berkeley, CA : Counterpoint, [2017]
Identifiers: LCCN 2017005020 | ISBN 9781619029354 (paperback)
Subjects: | BISAC: FICTION / Literary.
Classification: LCC PS3552.A244 S49 2017 | DDC 813/.54--dc23
LC record available at https://lccn.loc.gov/2017005020

Grateful acknowledgment is made to the following for permission to reprint previ-
ously published material: T.B. Harms Company: Excerpt from "Beyond The Sea" ("La
Mer") by Charles Trenet and Jack Lawrence. Copyright © 1945, 1946 Raoul Breton.
Copyright renewed 1973, assigned to T.B. Harms Company. Copyright © 1947 T.B.
Harms Company. Copyright renewed 1975, assigned to MPL Communications, Inc.
All Rights Reserved. Used by permission. Edward B. Marks Music Corporation:
Excerpt from "Manhattan" by Lorenz Hart and Richard Rodgers. Copyright ©
MCMXXV by Edward B. Marks Music Corporation. Used with permission. MPL
Communications, Inc.: Excerpt from "Beyond The Sea" ("La Mer") by Charles
Trenet and Jack Lawrence. Copyright © 1945, 1947 T.B. Harms Company. Copyright
renewed 1973, 1975 Whale Music Company, a division of MPL Communications, Inc.
International Copyright Secured. All Rights Reserved. Used by permission. Warner
Bros., Inc.: Excerpt from "Autumn in New York" by Vernon Duke. Copyright © 1934
Warner Bros., Inc. Copyright renewed. All Rights Reserved. Reprinted by permission.

Cover design by Kelly Winton
Book design by Domini Dragoone

ISBN 978-1-61902-935-4

COUNTERPOINT
2560 Ninth Street, Suite 318
Berkeley, CA 94710
www.counterpointpress.com

Printed in the United States of America

20 19 18 17 16

For Paul, Vicky, and Sarah

Three phases have succeeded each other during the span of my life. In the first the questions would be: "But who *is* she, dear? Who are her *people? Is she one of the Yorkshire* Twiddledos? Of course, they are badly off, very badly off, but *she* was a *Wilmot.*" This was to be succeeded in due course by: "Oh yes, of course they *are* pretty dreadful, but then they are terribly *rich.*" "Have the people who have taken The Larches got money?" "Oh well, then we'd better call." The third phase was different again: "Well, dear, but are they *amusing?*" "Yes, well of course, they are not well off, and nobody knows where they came from, but they are very *very* amusing."

—*An Autobiography,*
Agatha Christie (1894–1977)

PART I

Jacaranda

Jacaranda's name was pronounced "Jack-ah-*ran*-dah," as in jack-o'-*lan*-tern, the same rhythm. It's the name of a Central American flowering tree that grows in Los Angeles, and in Spanish it was originally "Hawk-ah-*rahn*-dah." It was just like her parents to name their daughter Jacaranda. Her father was a Trotskyite descended from bomb-throwing Russian anarchists, and Jacaranda's mother was born illegitimately, because *her* mother refused to marry the man who was the father. "I'm not marrying a rapist," Jacaranda's maternal grandmother explained. She moved to Texas and lost her illusions about the Catholic Church in one fell swoop—*she* was excommunicated, not *him!*

The Ocean

They lived in Santa Monica near the ocean. Jacaranda's father was a studio musician and they lived in a bungalow house, one with a mortgage, about two blocks from the ocean. Jacaranda grew up tan, with streaky blond hair, and tar on the bottom of her feet. Her sister, April, grew up three years younger, with a darker tan, and streaky reddish layers in her darker hair, and tar on the bottom of her feet. They looked absolutely nothing alike.

From the very start, Jacaranda was the big one with the large head who, till she was three, had to be swathed in pink for people not to say, "My, what a nice healthy boy you've got there . . ." April was a girl, a girlish girl with curly brown curls and a rosy-cheeked smile, delicate bone structure, and a small head. Neither Jacaranda nor April looked anything at all like the parents, Mort and Mae Leven, except that Jacaranda's head and Mort Leven's head were 7 ⅞ in hat size—one of the largest hat sizes, even for men.

The two girls grew up at the edge of the ocean and knew it was paradise, and better than Eden, which was only a garden. All Jacaranda cared about was surfing. First it was body-surfing where she would stare at the edge of the water, watching the waves to see which side the riptide was twisting back out on; then she'd slowly force herself upon the sea though it resisted. She'd walk out till she was up to her waist and all tangled up in the problem. The waves would now be coming and it was her choice, as they came, whether to slide on through under them in the glass-green water and ignore them crashing toward L.A. behind her—*or* to match herself up with the ocean's rhythm, to swim out just far enough, then stop, wait, push herself forward to catch the wave, and tumble into shore. Sometimes, if she miscalculated, she'd be swung back under the wave's lip and squashed down into the sand. When she was twelve, Jacaranda was given a surfboard.

No matter what the waves were doing, no matter what tides and thunders went on beneath her, she stayed on the board. The board tilted and tried to buck her off, the whole world slanted suddenly, the board would shoot out from under her before she knew it—the trick was to get the board back and keep going.

Jacaranda would surf before school and after school, and during school if she could, if the day was too nice. Mae Leven was "understanding" and would write notes to Jacaranda's teachers about her daughter "coming down with a cold." If Jacaranda tried it too often, Mae would turn into a black mamba snake and whirl around like a whip, snarling something darkly Southern.

Mort Leven played in the orchestra at Twentieth Century-Fox. They paid him $150 a week, which, in 1949 when he went "under contract," was a comfortable salary. It allowed him to put a down payment on their house in Santa Monica where they could live happily ever after for as long as ever after would bear up. Mort Leven's great-aunt Sonia was a major star in the early twenties and thirties, and two decades later was still so powerful with the studio executive system that she was able to get Mort a job. (In Hollywood, if you can't have a father in the Industry, the least you can have is a great-aunt.) It didn't matter that Mort

Leven had been a concert violinist or that he had studied with the greatest masters of his time and toured Europe; it didn't matter that he was probably one of the finest violinists in the world—not to Twentieth Century-Fox. What mattered to the studio was Sonia, Jacaranda's great-great-aunt and "godmother." Sonia was able to get Mort the interview with Harry Katz, the studio's chief musical administrator, an interview that in those days only a miracle or a father in the Industry merited.

Harry Katz had started out in the Yiddish theater on the Lower East Side and had a brother in the Industry, who in 1931 had sent for him to come out on a train to Hollywood. The pictures had sound and Harry could conduct the orchestra. After all, he'd been doing it since he was a kid in Toronto, a Jewish refugee like everybody else, a friend of Sonia's from "the old days" before Toronto, in Kiev. So "For Sonia's great-nephew, I put aside the official rules," he declared. "I let a total unknown try out in my office."

Mort was told to "bring something with a piano part" so Harry could play along and see just how well Mort could keep up. Mort Leven couldn't quite bring himself to debase his musical worth either. So he brought a piece, a new piece by Igor Stravinsky that he'd purchased in Paris, a piece that hadn't even been published in America yet, a piece where every measure was in a different time signature—so that it went from two-four to three-four (the waltz) to seven-eight to two-two to five-eight . . . Mort

Leven casually handed the piano part to Harry and, on a music stand, set up his violin score.

"Who is this guy Stravinsky?" Harry asked. "That how you pronounce it?" He opened the music, took one look at the time signatures, and burst into roaring laughter. "Is this a joke?" To Harry Katz, this was the funniest thing a job applicant had ever done—faked up a whole score of music this way! (Later, when Harry found out a certain Igor Stravinsky did exist, and was the musical genius of the century, and was the man who had just left Jacaranda's sixteenth birthday party with his glorious wife, Vera, he asked, "Morty, tell me the truth, a man like that, he can't be making more than twenty-five grand a year, can he?")

IT WAS AN easy life, growing up by the beautiful sea with her tan sister, her beautiful mother and black-curly-hair genius father, the Twentieth Century-Fox money rolling beautifully in every week, allowing Mort to save enough to buy real estate in Santa Monica. "Income property," it was called. (So many musicians at the studio had apartment houses and courts that the joke, one day, became "Tenants, anyone?")

In the days of her childhood, she was formally educated in three city schools where she mostly sat drawing pictures of Frederick's of Hollywood models dressed in comic-book high boots and masks, with garter belts, knives, and whips, with long wavy blond hair down to their waists in the back, cleavage in the front, and beauty marks dotting to the left of their left eyes. She had not been raised in any religion, though she assumed she was Jewish. She found matzah hidden underneath her grandparents' brocaded satin couch cushions, over at their West Los Angeles house every Passover. She really believed that the great religions of the world so far had come into being before anyone had grown up by the ocean. She believed in the ocean. Jacaranda believed that the ocean was a giant lullaby god who could be seduced into seeing things her way and could bring forth great waves. "Great waves, great waves, great waves," Jacaranda used to chant on bland days. On days when there were great waves, she would in silence bow her head toward the sea and thank it. She would talk to the water, implore it to hotten up. When the surf was hot, everything reached a state of hurling glory and perfect balance between her body and the tides and eternity. "You children who've grown up in California," she was often told, "you don't know what life is. One day you're going to run into a brick wall."

"Like what?" she asked. "Snow?"

Jacaranda spent the first summer after graduating from high school custom-painting surfboards for twenty-five dollars apiece in her parents' garage and bought a new old '59 Plymouth station wagon.

By the time she got out of Santa Monica High School, she was a spare figure out on the beach wearing torn blue shorts or a torn blue bikini. From afar, she looked as if she'd washed up on the shore, a piece of driftwood with blond seaweed caught at one end. She had calcium deposits on her knees and on the tops of her feet that were caused by the pressure of paddling huge older boards out into the ocean. (These bumps were called "surf bumps" and even the scientists down at the Scripps Institute in La Jolla didn't know exactly what they were.) From far away, she looked like all the other girls her age who were growing up near the water.

Up close, her expression—when she wasn't smiling—gave people the impression that she was brand-new—a child, almost. When she smiled, her perfect white teeth slashed the air with sudden beauty, giving her a glow of confidence that smacked of rude invincibility. ("Are those teeth real?" was the common question.) Her bangs were too long (down to her nose), making her eyes difficult to notice. (She'd always wished they'd been blue—blue the color of improved skies on postcards.)

Mae Leven used to watch Jacaranda and April come in from the beach at sunset, with their hair tangled and salty and their taut arms and legs dragging sand into the house behind them, and she'd coo, "Oh, there you are. My two string beans."

By the time Jacaranda was eighteen, she no longer looked like a boy, even with April standing right next to her.

People told Jacaranda she was lucky.

But luck is like beauty or diamond earrings: people who have it cannot simply stay home and receive compliments unless they've an enormous sense of public duty. Jacaranda wanted to see things before her luck ran out and she came upon the prophesied brick wall.

She imagined that she would be an adventuress and not need to go to UCLA or even Chouinard Art Institute, like Shelby Coryell, her one friend her own age. She would be an adventuress-painter, and just paint, because that's what she'd be good at. Blue was everything.

Outside, that first September, everyone had gone back to school and she had the whole empty beach to herself. Everything in the horizon looked clear and blue.

True Love

C olman didn't like the ocean.

"It's too cold," he explained, shuddering in his black turtleneck. "How can you go where it's too cold? That's why I left New York."

"Cold?" she said.

"*Cold*," he enunciated clearly.

But she was in love, so she moved in with him, way inland, to West Hollywood where he rented a ramshackle house all choked by passionflower vines. He had four ramshackle cats, named Harry, Dean, Stan, and Tentoes. His wife was divorcing him. He covered all his windows with black curtains because he hated the light in L.A., and daytime in general.

He had black curly hair and was plainly a genius—just like her father. He taught acting and everyone in his class said he was brilliant. He was twenty-nine and she was eighteen the night they met in Barney's Beanery, a ramshackle West Hollywood bar where she drank beer and flirted with artists at night. Barney's was one of the oldest bars in West Hollywood. Most of the artists were surfers who lived at the beach.

Colman was standing near the bar and his eyebrows went up gently when he saw Jacaranda. Everything Colman did made her laugh, and all he had to do was begin to tell a joke and she was lost.

After three weeks, Colman told her his wife had changed her mind about the divorce and was moving back in with him and bringing her cats, Fred and Rooster.

"More cats?" Jacaranda asked. "Your wife?"

He raised his eyebrows and spread his hands out in a "What can I do?" gesture.

Colman lied to her about everything and for a long time Jacaranda thought that that was what actors did offstage. But she found out most actors only lied for money in movies. He was entirely irresistible to all women, even Jacaranda's grandmother, who took one look at him and started blushing and afterward said, "The Irish are a lovely people."

"But, Grandma, you don't like Irish people because of their red hair, I thought."

"He has black hair," she said.

He was not too tall, five feet eleven, with pale Irish skin, and beautiful gracefully endearing eyes—there was nothing "wild Irish rose" about him. Even his lies weren't wild. His lies always leaned toward the tame. He lied that things were dull and lifeless without Jacaranda. If she asked him what was "new, terrific, and exciting," he'd sigh, yawn, and say, "Peace and quiet, my darling, just nothing but peace and quiet . . ." And she knew—three people would have told her—that he'd been with some starlet on the coats at a party the night before.

What she loved about Colman was his New York accent. He talked like a Dead End Kid. Ever since Jacaranda was little and first saw television, Leo Gorcey had been her idea of "a man." He was a lot like Mort Leven, but—instead of being Jewish—it was the Irishness that drove Jacaranda into peals of merriment; New York Irishness. New York Irishness was so exotic to Jacaranda that she had practically been able to overlook Elvis Presley's Southern comfort. Jacaranda always felt that one day far off in the future—when she got over whatever it was about Leo Gorcey that drove her so crazy—she'd be able to take a leisurely cruise through the South. She loved Southern accents, but at the very moment when she was melting away from the effects of one, Colman would telephone and say, "Hi ya, beauty, what's new, terrific, and exciting, huh?"

Being in love with Colman made her look beautiful. He loved her in purple and she wore purple clothes, which did her a lot more good than old shirts and torn shorts. Purple

eve babitz

made her hair look reddish golden and her skin look burning hot. She had a purple corduroy coat that would have stolen the show even on Rome's Via Veneto, where B-movie starlets paraded on summer nights in *La Dolce Vita*.

When Colman stood back, he could have been kissing her with his eyes, and Jacaranda knew what it was to be a palm tree who was truly adored, in lavender.

"Honey," Colman said, "do you love me?"

"Madly," she said.

He'd hand her some Red Hots, that cinnamon candy, and drive them farther up Laurel Canyon, because to him Laurel Canyon was a country road; he liked to drive out in the country.

Colman introduced her to all his friends, men who were junkies and actors and gamblers and cat burglars and jazz musicians. His idol was Chet Baker.

Colman had been depraved in his youth and understood entirely her desire to be depraved in her youth, too.

"Get it while you're young, kid," he said.

The best thing he told her, though, was in response to a remark she made about how two people they both knew couldn't possibly be married and oughtn't to be together. He said: "Honey, don't ever try to figure out what's going on between two people."

After she moved out of his house, he resumed life as a married man, and on the face of it it didn't seem right that they were still in love.

"But what will happen with Colman?" April asked. "How will it end?"

"End?" she said. "What would end it?"

For a while (five years) they met in an apartment in West Hollywood that belonged to one of Colman's students, Gilbert Wood, whom Jacaranda never met in all the years she and Colman spent afternoons there. She knew that Gilbert was an actor, that he sold marijuana, and that he kept his surfboard on top of his TV.

The Sixties

West Hollywood during the sixties, when life was one long rock-'n'-roll, was easy to live in with its $120-a-month two-bedroom apartment and landlords who were used to weirdness. Though there were such things as Families with Children and a Dog, most of the people who lived in West Hollywood were dope dealers, rock-'n'-roll musicians, road managers, groupies, waiters who were really actors but were writing screenplays in their spare time, and writers who were writing four screenplays each and collecting unemployment. Hairdressers, models who did commercials, and youngish people with no visible means of support, too, resided in that area, between Melrose and Sunset Boulevard, from La Brea to Doheny. In the sixties, West Hollywood was like an open city, a port at the crossroads of all directions.

Jacaranda offered to help a friend of Colman's out for a few days a week with his business. She circled and Xeroxed the names of all of his clients in the *Hollywood Reporter*, *Billboard*, and those "Teen Come" magazines, as she called them. And it more or less turned into a steady job. She made enough money to get her own West Hollywood apartment, gas, and drugs, and not have to be in a regular office where they expected her to wear shoes. Colman's friend, Hal, paid her $175 a week for going to rock-'n'-roll concerts and hanging around backstage, an occupation that her friends who were groupies thought was the luckiest thing they'd ever heard of.

She drank Southern Comfort with adorable rich young men who were often smart, and spent more and more nights up in those mansions above Hollywood and Beverly Hills where ambulances often lost their way and where handsome devils sat around on their amps trying to outdo each other in songs, blondes, and downers.

She went to the Monterey Pop Festival, though she never really remembered how she'd gone, come back, or what she'd done for the two days in between. Everyone took Sunshine acid and smoked grass called Icepack. And then, of course, there was all that tequila and rum and Courvoisier that rock-'n'-roll was finding out about after deciding grass wasn't enough.

She wore skintight satin pants and purple satin blouses. Her hair tangled down her back in blonder streaks of bleached disarray. She spent a lot of time in front of mirrors putting on brown eyeliner and mauve rouge, trying to see from behind her bangs, which still grew down to her nose and made her face look sweeter and more vulnerable when she was quiet and didn't smile.

"I hate rock-'n'-roll," she said, one night in the middle of the Stones at the Forum, and left.

HER SURFBOARD WAS lashed onto the top of her new old '59 Plymouth station wagon but she hadn't even been outside in the daytime, it seemed to her, since she took up with rock-'n'-roll. She was all white like an adult, not tan.

"I probably can't even stand up anymore," she moaned to April.

"Yeah, and it serves you right, too," April said.

"God, this thing is so heavy," Jacaranda complained, lugging her surfboard along to the beach near April's Santa Monica apartment. Jacaranda thought her lungs were going to rip.

She got to the water and touched it with her foot. It was February and wasn't very hot on the beach. But once Jacaranda was out where the waves broke, she found she could stand up and that her balance soon was intact. And she remembered how nothing else mattered.

"See, you can do it," April yelled from the shore.

April was now twenty, and because she was truly sympathetic to the human condition, she was besieged by a band of stars and handsome devils, who came to her when life for them stayed too glamorous for too long and didn't seem real. Eventually, April went to sea and became a sailor.

"I think I'll move back to the beach," Jacaranda said, panting and wet from throwing herself headlong into a battle of cold and tides. "I wonder if I still could make money painting surfboards."

They paused together to take one last look back at the ocean.

"God," Jacaranda said, "it'll be so nice to read a real book instead of the *Daily Variety*."

"Mother will be so relieved that you're going to settle down," April said.

"*Me?*" Jacaranda asked.

The Apartment

The apartment was in Santa Monica on Third Street, just a few blocks from the ocean, in a tumbling hillside alive with butterflies and cats. It was a long rectangle divided by two walls into a bedroom, a living room, and a kitchen. All three rooms looked straight out into a horizon of blue, gray, green Pacific with sunsets blazing orange in summer and glowing pink in winter. The bathroom was minute and the whole place had a rickety temporary attitude with a roof that leaked, but it only mattered when it rained and Jacaranda, being from L.A., thought the rain was more than a fair trade for damp rugs and puddles in the kitchen.

Three friends of hers from high school had opened the Eye of God Surf Company and offered to pay her thirty-five dollars per board for airbrushing tertiary and rainbow fades over the smooth surfaces of new boards.

The woman who rented her the apartment let her rent a garage in the back for twenty dollars a month where she could paint boards.

For the first six months, all she wanted was honest labor, finely crafted novels, and surf. She was clean again, for the ocean salt water was purifying and good for washing away the ravages of depravity.

"What's all that light doing in here?" Colman asked, on his first visit.

"It's from the windows," Jacaranda explained.

"But aren't you going to get sick of looking out at that ocean all the time?" Colman asked. "Look at this place, it's bright as day in here, how will you sleep?"

"You don't like my apartment," Jacaranda said.

"No, no, darling," he lied. "That's got nothing to do with it. I love this place. Really. I do."

She'd spent five whole years inland so that Colman could drop over in the daytime. She couldn't help it. She'd never told him this thing about herself but now he'd have to know.

"Colman," she burst out, "I usually wake up at seven. In the morning."

"Oh," he said. He thought about this, and then, "You mean, you sleep when it gets dark outside? At night?"

She'd only seen him in the afternoons when he'd just woken up, and naturally he assumed she had, too.

"Hey," he said, "did I tell you about this graffiti I saw in the men's room at the Knife and Fork? Someone printed: 'I'm ten inches long and three inches wide. *Interested?'* and wrote his phone number down. And then, in pencil underneath, someone *else* said, 'Fascinated. How big's your cock?'"

As Colman walked down the hill toward his old Buick, she knew he would have nothing more to do with her now that light was in her apartment.

The next day she found Emilio, a black satin cat with ambitions that seemed more peaceful than the ones alive in Colman or West Hollywood. Emilio specialized in patches of sunshine and sharpening his claws on her one chair and purring if she so much as uttered his camellia name, "Emilio."

About fifty of her friends continued to speak to her after she turned against rock-'n'-roll and they braved Olympic Boulevard down to the wilds of Santa Monica (not the beach her friends meant when they said "the beach"; they meant Malibu).

"I don't know," most of her friends said, "it's so far . . ."

"From what?" Jacaranda asked.

"The Troubadour, Tana's, everything!" they replied.

Jacaranda didn't care if rock-'n'-roll *was* the pulse beat of art in America, or a massive connection to everyone her age, or the background wallpaper of a generation that didn't seem to be dropping off and giving in to Frank Sinatra. She was tired of it.

"Maybe you're turning into an adult," April suggested.

"Me?" Jacaranda cried.

Surely there was something one could do besides becoming an adult just because she didn't want to live in West Hollywood or stand in a crush of eighteen thousand people at the Forum, listening to a white boy making all that money singing "Love in Vain."

But what?

"Will you feed my cat for me next week?" Jacaranda asked.

"Where are you going?" April asked.

A week later, Jacaranda boarded the plane in Oahu.

The Innocent Virgin

Jacaranda had taken the plane to Oahu to catch the smaller plane to Maui. She felt as if life contained nothing but odds and ends. She had always presumed that once people got to be twenty-three, they were Too Old, yet she was not old enough to content herself with brooding over the past like Marcel Proust, whose book she was reading on the plane, and who obviously had nothing more pressing to do than regard the years as a museum filled with beautiful reproductions of lost jealousy and bygone fashion. In another sense, she felt herself to be an Innocent Virgin—too young.

And so she began to see that instead of life becoming subdued as in Jane Austen novels, things were not to be that simple. Maybe the sixties had been too much for life ever to be that simple again. But rock-'n'-roll was behind her. And beneath her was the blue, blue sea.

She was wearing white jeans and a white Mexican blouse with a big pink silk rose pinned to it. She had only brought very little with her; she knew someone would loan her a surfboard.

The air felt funny when she landed, humid and ominous. They said a hurricane was on its way and that all inter-island planes for Maui were canceled.

In the Honolulu airport Jacaranda bumped into Shelby Coryell, her old boyfriend from the beach. He was in the airport to pick up some air freight. He'd graduated from Chouinard Art Institute and, she'd been told, had gone to the islands for a two-week vacation the year before but had never come home. He was still out in the water in Hawaii.

"I'm living with a girl on the North Shore," he said, "at Sunset Beach."

"Oh," she said.

How *dare* he live with someone, she thought as they drove off to Shelby's motel. She had always planned that Shelby would end up as hers. She decided to pull herself together and take him home to L.A. where he belonged, but when she got to his motel, she went for a walk on Sunset Beach, and there was Gilbert Wood.

In the hurricane, while everyone was home drinking rum and listening to ham radios about rooftops and towns being lifted out to sea, Gilbert Wood was surfing.

The waves were fifteen feet high and roared like lions and volcanoes. Gilbert Wood just crouched farther down on his surfboard and flattened his feet more. His left side, the side parallel to the waves, tilted slightly to enable him to drag his hand along inside the water, which left a white trail behind him the way his surfboard did, two white trails of foam and folly. He used his hand to practically confound the ocean, the day, and the hurricane. He was like a great beauty reaching for a cigarette in an officers' club.

And he was a great danger. He had ashy-colored hair, and in profile one side of his face was vicious. His mouth looked as though he'd just been hit with the news that he had a week to live and he didn't care.

Gilbert was an actor; he knew every last detail perfectly, of how beautiful he was. He was vain about danger, for hurricanes don't care if one is an actor or beautiful.

•

ON THE PLANE going back to L.A., Gilbert said, "Have you met Max yet?"

"Max who?" she asked.

Gilbert did two things that impressed her. One was to bite the back of her neck with his sharp teeth so that time stood still. The other was to introduce her to Max.

Max

Once Max noticed her, the only truth was Max's truth. At Gilbert's every morning at seven, the phone would ring. It would be Max. The first time this happened, Gilbert talked for a whole hour, laughing away throughout. Jacaranda asked, "Who was that at this hour?"

"Oh, just Max," Gilbert said, closing back up into his vain and dangerous self. There they were, in Gilbert's apartment—the place she and Colman had always gone to before she left West Hollywood forever.

"Max?"

"Just some fag I met at Jerry Getz's opening," Gilbert said.

Max noticed Jacaranda a whole month before she noticed him. She didn't know that Max was bristling with curiosity over her affair with Gilbert, but it was, in fact, Max's intense desire to uncover Gilbert's secrets that kept Gilbert so wrapped up in Jacaranda. Before Max showed up, she and Gilbert would not have lasted together more than two days after they had returned from Oahu, and now it had dragged on for a month, with Gilbert insisting Jacaranda come over every night, and Jacaranda doing what Gilbert said, because he was so dangerous and there was something mysterious going on that she couldn't figure out. She'd never have guessed it was just Max.

"I invited Max up for coffee," Gilbert announced one Sunday morning. Up until this point, it didn't seem as though she was debauched at all, but the truth was that while she believed in being a washed-up piece of driftwood on the shore, she also believed in bold adventuresses, cigarettes, and suffered from one too many of anything. It was one of those "Oh, no, I couldn't have" mornings for her again—not that Gilbert ever noticed. (One of the ways Gilbert cramped her style was by not noticing anything.)

"You invited him up for coffee?" Jacaranda asked.

"He wanted to meet you," Gilbert said.

"Me?" she asked.

"He's here," Gilbert said.

She looked at herself in the mirror. She looked a picture of health.

Then she heard him, Max.

MAX WAS A carburetor backfire in the driveway, an old green Jaguar with wooden paneling inside, and a dog named Diogenes. (Jacaranda thought, Diogenes! Really!) He emerged out of the Jaguar like a tall drink of water, like Cooper in *Morocco;* all he needed was a palm frond and a straw fan and he'd be complete. But he wasn't in the French Foreign Legion and he, by no means, told the limpid, careless innocent truth the way it was spoken by Gary Cooper (because Cooper was too lazy to do otherwise). Max's truth was sharpened by the sportsman honing of an artist whittler; like that Balinese carver's reply to the question about Art, "I just do everything as well as I can," Max just did truth as well as he could—he turned truth into a game, an art, when most others would just let truth pass by.

He was about six feet three and he had bright golden hair, a golden mustache, and eyes that reminded Jacaranda of those improved postcard skies. His face was lean and his mouth was pale, his teeth were vampiric—a tiny touch too long, but not from age. His neck was a slender Lucas Cranach neck and his body was slender; every move he made was like spring water, clear and salt-free. He wore white tennis shoes, white jeans, a white cotton shirt, and a red bandanna. Max saw her staring at him from inside Gilbert's window and, with one simple smiling motion, he bowed.

"You're *here!* Jacaranda Leven, right?" he drawled. (Oh—but a high-class sort of Savannah drawl from before Georgia was marched through, a drawl hardly extant in this world of redneck sentiments.) "I've heard so *much* about you."

Jacaranda said, "Oh . . . and I so little of you."

"Gilbert's a fine man," Max said, "but I'm afraid that boy's a little short on character assessment."

Jacaranda should have dumped Gilbert's "character assessment" of Max out the window, but instead she was thinking how sad it was that Max was a "fag" and what a pity it was that she would never be able to seduce him. He was so beautiful and that bow had made her eyes go dry, she'd forgotten to blink for so long. Perhaps what kept Jacaranda thinking Max was a fag was that there could be no other reason but a sexual one, in her opinion, for anyone at all to like Gilbert. He was without redeeming social value except for sex—Gilbert with his mean ash-green eyes and his monosyllabic replies and his rudimentary manly desires to climb Mount Everest and swim the Dardanelles.

Instead of ignoring Gilbert's "just Max" character assessment, Jacaranda resigned herself to Max being a fag. Maybe it was because she'd never tried to think what being a fag meant and what Gilbert's idea of a fag could be. Gilbert might regard the whole world as a panorama of worthless rubble, peopled by macabre perverts and Cro-Magnon women, from the way he spoke of them. But once she resigned herself to Max being a fag, she saw Oscar Wilde in every move he made.

Or maybe it was because she had never met a man who was passionate about elegance. What went on between men and women was based on a kind of enraged foundation that to Jacaranda could only be transcended through clashes-by-night sex. One of the things that made her laugh so much around Colman was the ridiculous distance between his grim dislike of his wife (and Jacaranda too) and his feelings that he was a prisoner of sex—and his love of his innocent lust. It was all balance. But then, she already knew that from surfing.

As Max sat there, his eyes occasionally landing on Gilbert, who was talking on the phone by the kitchen, it struck her that Max was fascinated by a death-defier like Gilbert for the same reason she was, out of sheer childlike amazement.

Gilbert's apartment was furnished by his landlord in cocoa-brown threadbare fifties' Modern with a cocoa-brown shag rug and stucco walls, which had been swirled into a pattern so life would be more interesting. He had a coffee table with cigarette burns on it and a pile of scripts with dust on top of them. His cast-off clothes were piled up in a high heap by the front door, waiting for him to remember to take them to the laundry. There was no door between the bedroom and the living room. His bed was a twisted torment of sheets, which he'd been meaning to change for two months. A vaseful of dead flowers, roses, stood on the windowsill. It was West Hollywood, all right, and the only thing that really was not indigenous was Max, his long fingers shaking out a match from lighting his and Jacaranda's cigarettes like some sort of lost art.

"Have you known Gilbert long?" Jacaranda asked, watching their smoke lured out the window by the sun.

"Have *you*?" he asked. He raised his eyebrows in elegant curiosity with a sort of stillness, an attitude of delight.

It was as though at last he'd found her and now they had nothing else to do but spend the rest of their lives discovering the mysteries of each other's perfection. The joy that came spilling off the way Max's shoulders drew toward her in rapt attention was the joy she knew they meant by something being "bigger than both of us."

"I haven't really known Gilbert that long," she said, "but I'm real close to his apartment."

"Gilbert," Max said, with a brilliant smile, "has the finest instinct for interior decoration in West Hollywood."

She didn't feel like laughing exactly, though what rose up in her was glee; she felt if only she and Max could sit this way, their cigarette smoke spiraling forever and Gilbert just inside their sight—well, if only they could.

Gilbert got off the phone. Instead of feeling, as she'd supposed she might feel, that Max would wreck her Sunday and that she'd want him to leave, she felt as though Gilbert were crude and inept. Gilbert's dangerous face, at that point, looked almost stylized, like a mask.

Once she noticed Max, everything else seemed only half true.

"Who was that?" Max asked. "On the phone?"

"Sandy Ryder," Gilbert said, pouring himself some more coffee.

"Oh," Max said, and a look crossed his face that was so sad and polite that one might think he was at a funeral and Sandy Ryder was the body.

"He's not so bad," Gilbert said. Jacaranda had never heard Gilbert say that someone wasn't so bad. She thought it was a trick.

"Not so bad!" Max cried, so excited he stood up and scowled. "Do you know what he said? Last time I saw him he told me: 'Truth is like old brandy; it should only be brought out late at night among close friends.'"

Max stepped on a ceramic ashtray in his indignation, striding to the window.

Gilbert looked innocent. He'd tricked Max into anger. "Truth should be carried like a banner before you!" Max went on.

"But don't you have any secrets?" Jacaranda asked.

"Secrets?" he replied. "Secrets are *lies* that you tell to your friends."

He turned to look out the window and she saw his profile against an enormous bush, blooming with white oleanders. Her mother had always warned her about oleanders; they were poisonous and one was never to eat them.

The white flowers threw Max's elegant silhouette into a sort of bas-relief, like Ghiberti's Gates of Paradise, in Florence, golden. The sunshine was golden. The cigarette smoke and coffee smelled golden.

Max sighed, paused a moment, and then turned to her. "Are you coming tonight?" he asked.

"Coming?" she asked.

"Didn't Gilbert invite you? I'm having a few people over. For drinks. I'm at the Sacramento. Wear anything."

Diogenes was yawning and wagging and then Max was outside, a loudly backfiring carburetor, backing out of the driveway, and silence.

All that remained were the dead roses on the window and Gilbert, who raised one eyebrow crossly like a brown-haired child who won't eat.

"Amazing, isn't he?" Gilbert said.

He got to his feet and then, suddenly, crude, stylized Gilbert, with his flat-footed crouch and his vanity and his doomed mouth, turned into Max, languid and intense, with Max's fancy drawl.

"Secrets," he said, "are *lies* that you tell to your friends!"

Jacaranda gathered together the broken ashtray, so no one would get cut, as she wondered what she'd wear that night, now that everything was going to be perfect.

The Little Black Dress

She wore a little black dress, which in a mad dash she had borrowed from April. It was the kind of little black dress that Mae Leven always described as "decent." April and Mae had found it on one of their perpetual treks out to Pasadena where two city blocks were lined with Salvation Army–type thrift stores. This little black dress cost $3.49 and was a Dior. With the jacket, it could be worn to court or to a funeral. Without the jacket, it was no longer quite so decent and Jacaranda was sure it would be the right thing to wear around someone like Max, who was ten years older than Gilbert (Gilbert was two years older than she). With little gold sandals, the dress was fine.

She spent about an hour in the bathtub crooning "I'm So Lonesome I Could Die" to her black cat Emiliano (his nickname, after she remembered *Viva Zapata!*).

She brought fresh flowers in from the tumbling-down hill where her landlady threw handfuls of wildflower seeds each spring. She stuck the wildflowers into a glass; and sang her entire repertoire of Hank Williams songs, which she had only recently begun to appreciate.

In the little black dress, with its square neckline and Paris, France, drape, she looked all wrong in L.A., especially in her old station wagon with surfboards on top. But if she'd been in Paris or Rome or New York, she'd have looked smart.

It wasn't until it was too late that she realized she had only a large straw purse and not the little clutch purse the dress called for. On the phone April said, "A what?"

"A clutch purse," Jacaranda repeated.

"*Me?*" April said.

Jacaranda's hair was even blonder after Hawaii and her skin was tanner than usual. She painted her toenails grape, which matched her eye shadow. Her eyes, lined in brown pencil, looked out with innocent-virgin deception and complemented her large mouth with its expression of eager vulnerability. Her hair, parted in the middle, hung straight down untangled.

She looked as though she'd just stepped out of an opening-night intermission in London and not at all as if she lived on a hill apartment in Santa Monica with a roof that leaked.

Outside, the ocean was spread out in a blue line, and the sun, an orange circle, hung just above it, about to set.

She sang "Your Cheatin' Heart" all the way into Hollywood.

The Sacramento Apts.

The Sacramento was smack in the middle of Hollywood—the neighborhood called Hollywood, not the mystical state. It wasn't in Beverly Hills or West Hollywood, which were both All Right, and it wasn't down by the beach or in Trousdale or Bel Air or Encino, which were all All Right, too. It was in Hollywood, smack in the middle, which was not All Right. It never was All Right, even back in the twenties when Valentino, an unknown, got all dressed up and strolled down Hollywood Boulevard, hoping to be noticed and put into a movie.

Of course, a few New York types thought "the Coast" was simply "the Coast" and that it didn't make any difference where one stayed because it was only for two weeks and then one could go home to civilization, New York. And she'd heard they stayed in the Sacramento, which was why several New York comedians telling jokes about "the Coast" used to talk about Hughes Market, a block away from the Sacramento, a market nobody from L.A. ever went to because it was too expensive.

But for Max to be in the Sacramento meant it had been misunderstood and that it, and the part of Hollywood it was in, were both perfectly fine, after all.

It was one of those apartment-hotels with a lobby and a front desk and a manager, an elevator, thick walls, and high ceilings. Max lived in the penthouse, or what he called the penthouse, though it was hard for most people to think of a five-story building as having a penthouse.

It was eight, exactly, when she knocked on his penthouse door.

The door was flung open.

"You're *here!*" Max said, his blue eyes alight with how wonderful she was. "You *dressed!* You look marvelous. The best-dressed woman in Los Angeles!"

"Except for the purse," she said, showing him her car keys and cigarettes, which she'd brought along in her hand.

Max was still tall and wore a caramel-colored polo shirt and denim pants that were almost, but not quite, jeans that were white. He wore espadrilles that were worn out. Everything about him looked clean and bright. His hair, which was still wet, had been combed back off his face but the same strand that fell down when it was dry had already begun falling, wet or no. He smelled like a birthday party for small children, like vanilla, crêpe paper, soap, starch, and warm steam and cigarettes.

Anyone would have liked being hugged by him.

Only she, so far, had arrived. But there was a folly of luxury the likes of which Jacaranda couldn't believe. There it was smack in the middle of a geography that was All Wrong. (If she'd come in later through the back parking lot, she would have seen limousines lined up—limousines looking startled at slumming in such an unlikely spot. Hollywood wasn't exactly a slum—it was just Not Right.)

"I'm just fixing the salad," Max said. "Tell me what you think."

On a buffet of white-tablecloth tables were the most beautiful dishes, all white, with stainless-steel Italian-designed silverware (a little finer than anyone else's silverware, she noticed). There were perfectly folded and ironed white napkins, and white ceramic pots filled with white flowers. There were wineglasses and Scotch glasses and gin-and-tonic glasses. The bottles, all Windexed into a high gloss, stood full of Scotches and gins and sherries and vodkas, and there were white wines in the refrigerator and red wines open and out. The wooden floor was polished and glowing beyond the rug and the whole penthouse was without a trace of grime or dirt anywhere.

There was art all over the walls. Jasper Johns, Rauschenberg, a David Hockney swimming pool, and a huge pornographic watercolor by John Altoon. In the front to the right, where people came in, was a carefully framed photograph by Julian Wasser of Marcel Duchamp playing chess with a naked girl. The contrast between Duchamp's dried-out ancient little person and the large young girl's Rubenesque flesh was not (unlike chess) at all subtle. This photograph was the only thing on Max's walls that people actually looked at; even Altoon's pornography was a little too tasteful to arouse real interest.

"You've got a print of this," she said, her voice filled with hurt surprise. She'd never imagined that anyone might *own* a print and not have to tear it out of an art magazine as she had had to do.

"You *know* this photograph?" Max asked.

"Well, I mean . . ." (She'd have to be an idiot to spend all her time around artists and not know *this* photograph.)

"How would a friend of Gilbert's know Duchamp?" Max said.

"Yes," she said, looking at him now, "how would you?"

"Gilbert is a wonderful person," Max said, "but I just didn't think . . . Well, how do you like my apartment?"

"Why have you done this to the poor Sacramento?" she asked.

"What do you mean?" he said.

"Turned it into . . . the Plaza Hotel," she said, taking a stab at it, since it looked exactly as she imagined the Plaza Hotel must look.

"Oh," he said, turning to look at her with deep seriousness for the first time since they'd met, holding her in his gaze, "how *won*derful you are!"

The doorbell rang.

"How wonderful *you* are," she replied, smiling.

He looked at her just once over his shoulder from the front door, which he was about to open, and the whole world was filled with questions before them. The bell rang again.

"You're *here!*" he cried.

"Darling!" someone said. "Is this Hollywood?"

Max's laugh was like a dragnet; it picked up every living laugh within the vicinity and shined a light on it, intensified it, pitched it higher. It was a dare—he dared you not to laugh with him. He dared you to despair. He dared you to insist that there was no dawn, that all there was was darkness, that there was no silver lining, that the heart didn't grow fonder by absence. He dared you to believe you were going to die—when you at that moment knew, just as he did, that you were immortal, you were among the gods.

JACARANDA COULDN'T QUITE remember when it was that she had glided from the banks of the Nile onto the barge. Perhaps because even that first night nothing had looked very different from the rest of the world. Well, of course, things were a little finer at Max's, better silverware. Ease. But other than that, she saw nothing different; after all, it wasn't as if money had been poured into the place, or that money was no object.

It was just that Max, and all of Max's things, were so carefully chosen—like his friends—so perfect. Other than a sort of seamless wicked, sarcastic, teasing temperament about it all, one could hardly tell the barge was moving. Or that there was a Nile.

Or that on the banks of the Nile an unfortunate population was forced to go through life with brick walls and learned lessons, rather than simply float while catching tossed grapes, until with practice, one day, it became habit.

There was something special about Max's parties, those first two years at the Sacramento, that she could never think about afterward without condensing it into one particular night.

As usual, in those days, the people who were from Los Angeles entered doubtfully, unsure about the Sacramento and wondering who Max was and what he wanted and why he'd invited them.

Within the first few moments after they'd arrived, they'd be drenched in Max's delight with them and everything would become smooth and golden, and soon (this was what Jacaranda afterward never forgot) the whole place would ascend to heaven.

Max's food was divine. His guests—all his other guests suddenly realized—were simply pillars of kindness, goodness, and beauty. The napkins were so fresh and bright. The salad was springtime in each bite.

"Have you seen his ice thing?" a guest might ask another.

"Ohhh," the second guest would say, "isn't it beautiful?"

And all it would be was an ice cooler, the kind one can buy in Milan, just slightly better than an ordinary ice cooler.

On this particular night, Jacaranda's first, Max's penthouse had filled up and people were sitting everywhere, humming and purring, a tight golden roll running through the air.

Gilbert was standing, leaning against the same wall that Jacaranda leaned against, and the two of them had been watching in smooth dreamy pleasure for nearly twenty minutes, not saying a word to each other. Finally, Gilbert cleared his throat.

"You know," he said, "I think we ought to petition the Pope for a special dispensation—a year's suspension of disbelief."

When Jacaranda began to laugh, Gilbert turned and looked at her with an expression of puzzled concern, as though he didn't know what was so funny.

Gilbert's eyes were sometimes so green, but he was an actor. And Jacaranda just couldn't be around someone who might be discovered, become a star overnight, and turn into a property. She rarely saw Gilbert alone after meeting Max, but she often was alone with Max.

The Barge

Max had two kinds of friends.

Jacaranda was in the handful of people he took up with because he was in Los Angeles.

But the main group belonged in the world, and were not tied down to any particular geography. They were mostly the names you read in *W* and on lists at weddings in *Vogue* or *Queen*, only instead of being in black-and-white, they were in color and moved. And instead of looking extremely uneasy and "public," they looked extremely relaxed and protected. A childhood of privacy seemed to buffer them against the cruel fates of flash bulbs. Max gathered these public people and, through his laughter and money and his "amusing" penthouses, he brightened their lives and made the simplest things seem framed in gold. The women who organized charity bazaars, operas, festivals, and museum openings just fell into Max's open "You're *here!*" arms. ("You're *here!*" was how he greeted every single guest at every single party Jacaranda ever saw him host—Max was a host: it was in his genetic code.) "You're *here!*" he'd delight, and into his arms would fall an elegantly poised lady, suddenly a child of sorrow and joy, who'd say, "Oh, thank God, Max, yes, I *am!*"

They all knew where they all ate in Paris and where to go to in New York and whom to see if they went to Stockholm and they referred to each other as "dear friends."

They demanded the same French food (what Jacaranda called "kosher fillet of sole") in every city on earth, and were suckers for going to bars and nightclubs and restaurants because their "dear friends" went, no matter how much better the place next door was. They were perfectly ready to talk about airports for hours and not be bored.

When Jacaranda realized that these people were the ones meant by the words "jet set," she was sure there must be a mistake. Why travel if it's always going to be fillet of sole every night? If it hadn't been for Max, the "dear friends" would have been stuck with each other in French restaurants forever.

But then, most people like even bad French restaurants. They're used to them. And besides, one can always compare the food to the way it ought to have been, because one *knows*. French restaurants are not like art or love, after all; they're like money, standard.

The women in this group were never quite in the mood for Los Angeles and often got tired in one day of Rodeo Drive and shopping. Besides, they had done it all before. Now and then, they would turn to Jacaranda and say, "You live here, don't you? How can you live in L.A.? What do you *do*?"

The men all wanted to become movie producers and questioned her on what she thought they should do in order to make movies.

"Get some film," she said once.

The idea that these people spent their whole lives outside of the movie business seemed exotic to her, but by the time she realized that the "dear friends" only recognized each other, and only ate French food, and would never have known her had it not been for Max, it was too late, because by that time she knew that fillet of sole is usually the safest bet. And that in general, as far as groups of strangers were concerned, the "dear friends" were probably the least impossible.

JACARANDA THOUGHT OF the "dear friends" living on a drifting, opulent barge where peacock fans stroked the warm river air and time moved differently from the time of everyplace else. Everything was better on the barge, the same kind of ease seemed to scent the nights. The barge passed through cities, along the countryside, and through major events without ever disturbing the thick layer of ease between it and the rest of the world. Perhaps the reason was that, surrounded by the Nile as it was, the barge was protected from most disturbances by hungry crocodiles waiting, like logs, in the river.

Max, Max

People said that his family paid him six thousand dollars a month to stay out of Alabama. Others said that he was just rich, pure and simple. Jacaranda never saw Max do anything but empty ashtrays and cook. When she first knew him, Jacaranda asked, straight out, "Max, do you do something, or what?"

"'Do?'" he replied. "You mean like work?"

"Sort of," she said. She'd read, of course, that people with manners never asked other people how they got money, but she didn't believe it.

"Well," Max said, "I do a little bit of this and a little bit of that, you know."

"*What*, though?" she insisted.

There was a rumor that, as a sort of "social director" for the Beautiful People on the barge, he was kept in finery and not allowed to worry his pretty head about money; that his friend Etienne Vassily (and God knew where *he* came from) paid for everything.

Jacaranda could not even figure out how much money he'd have to have to live in the Sacramento and smell like vanilla and have Duchamp on the wall, and white ironed napkins. Sometimes she got the impression that he was just a figure in a landscape who began moving into the festivities the instant he knew someone was looking.

But other times she felt very, very close to him and heard him breathing and saw exactly what he saw and knew exactly why he did things and understood everything without a hitch. When he cooked in his kitchen, she forgot to wonder about who Max was and was overcome with instinct as she anticipated every move he was going to make and brought him the right wire whisk and herb or spice and put it nearby where he would find it easily.

Most of the time, Max wasn't even in L.A. He was in New York where, he said, "They're so provincial."

Max usually served food so delicious that for itself alone people could have gone home satisfied. There needn't have been unending champagne, fellow guests who seemed hand-picked to transport you into the kind of heaven you loved best, or Max himself, who never let the ball drop for a moment, and was always ducking in and out of silences, laughing at how brilliantly things were going. You could have just had the food and gone home happy.

He always made everything himself, and when Jacaranda was in the thick of the barge's evenings, she'd go early to Max's and watch. (When Etienne Vassily was handling things, servants were imported who knew how, or else he brought them with him and installed them in the servants' bedrooms of his "bungalow" mansion. Once he brought ten along for a special nerve-racking occasion to entertain forty people who had been invited to stop by around eight for "something to eat and a chat." Etienne relied on simple opulence like fresh caviar to settle the question of food.) Watching Max cook was when Jacaranda came closest to thinking Max came from someplace, had a childhood, and might have brothers or sisters, sisters especially.

"Where *are* you from?" she asked once while Max was expertly measuring out olive oil for salad dressing.

"The Old South," he drawled.

"Come on," she said.

"Louisiana," he replied. "Really. That's where I was really born and lived till I ran away."

"My mother's from Louisiana!" Jacaranda said.

"Your mother." Max shrank back as though from a loud cannon noise. "That woman. My stars."

"You're the only man I've ever known who didn't fall in love with my mother," she observed.

Max loosened up and set about chopping thin slices of celery.

"Mmm," he said.

He chopped celery like a Chinese professional.

Max knew so well what he was doing in that kitchen at the Sacramento that Jacaranda seldom intruded until it came time to wash the dishes the next morning. (The morning following most of those parties, Jacaranda stopped by to help Max and listen to his version of the night before.)

But it was the food, as far as she was concerned, not the heavenly other events at Max's, that was really the center. Max's salads were always more beautiful and kinder than anyone else's salads; he never put too little or too much vinegar or anything untoward like honey into the dressing. All the leaves were gloriously green and fresh and crisply eager, except for the watercress, which held back and added character and shadow. His French bread was always the exact right warmth and freshness, straight from the French bread store in Beverly Hills. And he usually made rose potatoes or rice to take care of anyone who wanted another starch. His rice was always perfect. Steamed. Most of the time he made light dishes out of chicken or fish because he had taken so much acid that eating red meat stopped him cold, and because he didn't know anyone who wasn't on a diet. (Except Etienne, but Etienne could always eat cold roast-beef sandwiches when he got back to the bungalow, and always did.) The best thing Max made, Jacaranda thought, was red snapper poached in white wine, olive oil, and butter, with snow peas and translucently sliced onions and mushrooms. (He thought mushrooms were a horrible affectation of the middle class and he hated the middle class's sad attempts to attain elegance.) The second-best thing Max made was chicken sautéed in tarragon and butter, with fresh parsley sprinkled over the top. Jacaranda loved tarragon. Perhaps it was the way Max served food, and not the food itself, for the way an orange tasted if Max had handed it to her was better than any orange she'd eaten before.

JACARANDA OFTEN HEARD about Etienne Vassily. People were surprised that she hadn't met him.

"You mean," someone would ask, "you know Max but you don't know Etienne?"

If Max was nothing more than one of Etienne's paid amusements, like a dance band, a servant, then he was obviously the best. Nobody cooked half so well.

It was one of the basic wonders of Max's personality in those first two years that he could tell her, "You are the best-dressed woman in L.A.," or that New Yorkers were "provincial," with such glee that it was dazzling and somehow tender-hearted.

Social Direction

U ntil the night, at a black-tie supper for sixty for the opening of the Venice Biennale, when Etienne first met Max, Etienne's ambitious practical jokes had an unfortunate likelihood of being unforgivable. This interfered with Etienne's main ambition—to take over the world.

Max and Etienne sat down as strangers to dine in formal splendor and before dessert, slipped out as dear friends. They left the party together and it was discovered that they'd taken off in Etienne's plane. For three days and nights they were "missing"—even the plane radio had been shut down. News that Etienne was dead did beady-eyed little things to the stock market. (News that Max was "missing" was simply not news, since he was never supposed to be anywhere.) Finally, Etienne's third wife caught up with them. They were in jail in Kyoto for lewd conduct; they'd been found naked tied to an orphanage post and were being beaten by little girls, with real whips, who were trying hard to draw blood (it was reported), flogging their best.

". . . and my husband didn't even go on to the art opening," Etienne's third wife testified as she told the judge the mental torment she'd undergone that made her demand a divorce and a cool million, though they'd only been married for two months. The judge in Kyoto was understanding and let Etienne off with a warning not to get caught doing that again. The judge in New York gave Etienne's third wife $100,000 and told her that a woman who marries a man of Etienne's reputation doesn't deserve a penny more for just two months.

Once Etienne met Max, he could devote himself to taking over the world and know that the half of him that only wanted to play was being fully seen to, and could be dished up, unimpeded by last-minute lack of plans, like a flaming shish kebab in a cornball tourist trap. Max, it was said, was simply brought in as Vice-President in charge of the Latin-American press for one of Etienne's Venezuelan companies that lost money and would now lose a fortune owing to the high cost of Max's salary—it supposedly dovetailed into some kind of tax loop that was more beautiful, almost, to Etienne than Gelsey Kirkland. Etienne, it was said on the barge, could put any amount of money into this Vice-President's "entertainment fund" and it still made money for him.

Meanwhile, Max, like Michelangelo being given an open-ended budget by the Medicis, went ahead designing the architecture of particular places for Etienne, which were in as many cities as Max could arrange. Etienne liked different backdrops and colorful native customs. Etienne loved it, for example, that Jacaranda actually painted surfboards for a living. But Max, with his quick gaming eye, knew it was not even necessary that she paint surfboards for she was a rare enough thing—a native-born Angeleno grown up at the edge of America with her feet in the ocean and her head in the breaking waves, with a bookcase full of the kind of reading matter that put her in touch with the rest of the world. She was without any spiritual taint; she had neglected (she'd tried, but it was too boring) to read the Bible and, in fact, all religious books just failed to capture her imagination—she was without the "civilizing influence" that mankind has always enforced upon its young. She only knew about Adam and Eve the way a classical scholar immersed in Aristotle's *Ethics* would know that Liz and Dick were holding up production on *Cleopatra*—by passing the newsstand on his way to the coffee shop. She had no sense of "sin" and no manners. She was the way she was by the Levens' letting her alone to read, and she knew her way around Los Angeles like a Bedouin on his own two thousand square miles of trackless waste.

Max decided to arrange a meeting between Jacaranda and Etienne on the spur of the moment, one afternoon, when Max was visiting Jacaranda's and Etienne was in town. Max had been visiting Jacaranda every day for two months. Every day, around three, Max would "just drop by for tea or a beer, I've brought the beer," and every day, Jacaranda got more and more used to it. There Max would be. She couldn't get used to Max but she got used to his being there. Her heart still turned four golden beats whenever he stayed late and the sun would shine a certain way across his profile.

That day Max asked if Jacaranda minded if he used her phone. "I would like you to meet a friend of mine. But I'm going to play a trick on him. Is that O.K. with you?" Jacaranda's days had become *so* full of Max's tricks, his laughter and his blue, blue eyes, that naturally it was all right with her. She just waited, looking out the window at the smoggy afternoon, while Max dialed.

"Hello?" Max began, "You're *there!* . . . Listen, I want you to come over right away, it's important. . . . No, I met a woman in the supermarket. . . . Her husband is in . . . ["By the Time I Get to Phoenix" was playing across the street on someone's radio] Phoenix. So you've got to come at once. . . . No. Now. It's important; they'll understand. Here's the address. . . . I *know* it's far away from Beverly Hills. But she says she wants to meet you. She says she makes the best frozen potatoes au gratin in L.A." His eyes grew demoniacally bluer, impossibly bluer. "Of course if you can't make it . . ."—bluer still—"all right, then, we'll be expecting you."

"*I* don't look like a housewife!" Jacaranda protested. "He'll never believe this. Besides, there's no furniture."

It was true. Jacaranda had been living in the apartment for almost a year and all she had was Emilio. In the living room, she had two folding chairs and an orange crate on which to put the ashtray. Her clothes, in one of the back closets, were all of her really that was there. Except that the living room was pillared with a surfboard. It leaned against the wall, dry and waiting for the owner to come with the truck to pick it up.

Twenty minutes later, a new beige Lincoln Continental pulled up sharply across the street.

"He's here," Max said, lighting a cigarette.

"What do I *do*?" Jacaranda was wondering how her life had gotten so impossible when only last year she'd retired.

Out of the Lincoln stepped one of the most powerful men in the world.

He was about fifty years old and had thick gray hair that had been gracefully shaped so that his Byzantine classicism was visible. His eyes were rounded and dark, with black lashes, and his mouth was thick and dark red. He had a gray-black mustache and nice eyebrows, but his eyes, surrounded by their black lashes, were purple velvet. It wasn't fair, Jacaranda was always to think whenever she remembered seeing Etienne's eyes up close for the first time, that he had velvet purple eyes and *her* eyes were miserable brown. He was built like a lizard or a saluki. He was narrow and ancient-looking; his skin looked like papyrus, five thousand years old but not wrinkled, just from another age—from an age before they knew about chocolate or Dante or Charlie Chaplin. He was small, only five feet nine, with narrow shoulders, but his clothes were immaculate and his hand, when Jacaranda was offered it to shake, was as tempting and tended as though it had been kept fit for a king. His voice sounded abrasive, nervous, and his purple eyes darted around the apartment, never once looking at Max, while Max just stood leaning on one foot—a tall drink of water—waiting for Etienne to give up. But Etienne wasn't going to give up; he would assess every hint, every clue, every past iota of data, and finally the information would link up and he'd know everything. Etienne said, holding out his tended hand, "You are Jacaranda Leven."

Max, the joke on himself, nearly collapsed with laughter as he recounted, tears streaming down his face, the "potatoes au gratin" line and the "Phoenix" touch. But Etienne stood as still as a stag in a forest waiting for his own instinct, his *own* information, to come in as he looked at the surfboard, looked carefully at what was painted on the surfboard and how it was painted, looked with piercing exactitude; he looked at the no furniture, he looked at an open closet. He looked at Jacaranda and his judgment of how her skin would feel that night in the dark with the jasmine all around them was nearly perfect, except that he hadn't quite known she'd be *that* satiny—for women with skin as satiny as hers are not so easily found. His eyes slid to the back bedroom where bookcases lined all the walls to the ceiling and he saw, from a distance of thirty feet, a group of books familiar enough to him in their paperback form to recognize as he said, "I see you read C. P. Snow. What's a girl like you reading him? He doesn't know a thing about power." Etienne snapped, "Not *one* thing."

"Oh," Jacaranda said. She'd so hoped that reading C. P. Snow would tell her all she needed to know about the manipulations of powerful serious people so she wouldn't have to be such a provincial.

"Well . . ." Jacaranda sighed. "If that diamond ring don't shine . . ."

"I beg your pardon?" He formally cocked his head.

"What would you suggest I read?" she asked.

"Oh." He shrugged. "Max knows about books. I never read."

"What race are you from?" Jacaranda asked.

"The brown race," he told her, opening the white silk right side of his made-in-Milan jacket to take out a tortoise-shell cigarette case and offer her a cigarette, which he then lit with a gold Cartier lighter.

"What a pretty bunch of stuff," Jacaranda said.

"Like it?" he asked.

"I love it," she said.

"I give it to you," he said, laying the lighter and the ciga-rette case down on the orange crate.

"I really like the jacket," she said.

"I give that to you, too," he replied; a light in his purple velvet eyes began to burn. He was not bored. Fun. At last.

"What's your shirt made out of?" she asked.

"Do you like it?" he asked.

"No," she said.

"Perhaps you'll like the one I shall wear for you this eve-ning," he said.

"I don't really like shirts," Jacaranda confessed. "But thanks for the jacket, it's really beautiful."

"I'll send a car for you at seven o'clock. A few people for drinks. You know. Max will be there."

"What kind of car?" she asked.

"If you like it," he told her, "you may keep it."

"I'd rather drive myself," she said, "so if I want, I can escape."

The light went out and he was bored again. The word "escape" had blown out the glow: it was so *boring* of these American women to imagine they were worth pursuing.

"Send your car for me," she said, changing her mind.

"At seven, then," he replied, bowing at the waist, looking at his watch, nodding at Max, and out. He glided like a lizard. In his eyes the light was back on.

Max cracked the air with peals of laughter that followed Etienne down across the street and must have been heard a block away; the joke was on them all.

Max, Max, Max

Somewhere along the way, Max's tender-hearted, gleeful mastery turned to tears of poison.

Somehow, when Max one day said, "Jacaranda is the best-dressed woman in Los Angeles," it came out sounding mean-spirited and vile. The gold had washed off the surface and the Gates of Paradise had been melted down for private purposes no longer on public view. It was only art anyway, Max's attitude seemed to say—a dismissal of all he'd been before—and suddenly he smelled like suitcases and dry cleaning, not a birthday party for an eight-year-old at all. She kept waiting for him to change back.

Jacaranda, like most people who knew Max, had never been so close to anyone as she had been to him, and when he turned to poison, she, like even some of the worldly "dear friends," felt it wouldn't last, that it would resume being golden any day. She never knew why it didn't.

April

pril hated Max.

She loathed and despised Etienne.

April couldn't stand Jacaranda's infatuation with the lull of a river, the stupidity of a barge. The ocean was the sister's place, not some river, not people so safe and sound, all eating peeled grapes.

April became a champion of sewing sails and went to work in the Pacific ports. She bought a professional machine capable of surmounting tough canvas and needles that didn't snap piercing thick fabric.

April hated Max, though, the most.

"What are you *do*ing with those people?" she asked, the morning after she'd stomped out of Etienne's bungalow mansion, offended, in only an hour, by one of the usual vulgarities that had only just begun. Small vulgarities were enough to remove April from the tableau: "They're awful people!"

Bungalow Mornings

The parties would last till 2 or 3 a.m. The girls would tempt Etienne and he'd choose one, perhaps a pretty little laughing blonde he had besieged with dozens of roses, color TVs, and even diamond stud earrings—anything her little heart desired. They were high in Trousdale, hanging above L.A. with the jasmine. Although oleanders overgrew the gates, Etienne's oleanders were pink, not white. At about midnight, suddenly, the whole thing would become too boring and Etienne would start spewing insults at the little blonde. Or, worse yet, forget her and start fresh on some new woman who crossed his path.

Jacaranda, of course, being in love with Max, didn't care too much about Etienne's intentions (except it wasn't nice, what he'd said to April, so before that evening was finished Jacaranda poured pineapple juice all over his fresh cream silk suit). Since Jacaranda cared so little about what Etienne was doing, she usually wound up being the one with whom Etienne slept. By two or three o'clock, Jacaranda would be the only unpassed-out woman extant, and she, Max, and Etienne would have a nightcap and discuss the evening, until one of them was sent home in a Rolls-Royce limousine—Max.

Along with the opium, champagne, brandy, and cocaine, Jacaranda and Etienne would clash by night, sometimes till dawn, when they'd walk along the dewy lawns (she never knew whether he owned or rented this paradise) toward the view and watch L.A. turn blush pink, then yellow, then smog.

In the mornings at Etienne's, the phone would ring at seven o'clock, almost simultaneous with the coming of the smog, and it would be Max, who'd arrive in person fifteen minutes later. By that time, Etienne had showered and spoken long distance twice. He immersed himself in adult business and paced in small rectangles, small like his shoulders and bones, ancient little rectangles like Euclid discovering geometry. He'd jingle the coins—the francs and pesos and yen—in his dressing-gown pocket (for tips?), his abrasive voice snarling out commands as he drew farther and farther into the garden and away from Jacaranda and Max, who were in the midst of their daily arguments, which began the moment Max showed up, along with toast, coffee, and the servant saying "Anything else?"

Now and then, Etienne would turn from the oleanders and jasmine and give a bored shrug in their direction to tell them to keep their voices down, that what he was doing was *important!*

Jacaranda wondered if Etienne felt as if he were the put-upon father of two querulous children.

Jacaranda wondered if she and Max were married.

Jacaranda wondered if all marriages were like this.

And if they were like this, she wondered how long theirs could go on. She had taken to drink and grown slack. If it wasn't for the fact that she'd had such an iron constitution, she surely would have collapsed by then. She remembered the night that Lydia Antonia had almost expired in a sigh and had to be ambulanced away. Her condition had been diagnosed as simple malnutrition (Lydia, a "dear friend" who might at least have taken a bite of her fillet of sole once in a while). But Jacaranda kept muddling through, able to arise each morning looking just slightly tangled and confused, a look that was almost cute, especially when she frowned and moaned, "Oh, God! Oh, no. Oh, I couldn't have!"

As for Etienne, he seemed pleased with Jacaranda's bravado. It was as though the more pasty-faced and impossible she became with each passing month, the more it pleased him watching her drunkenly delude herself that she was sailing along, walking on water. Jacaranda's kind of foolhardy determination made Etienne's eyes grow madly hot. There was something in Etienne that made him sympathetic to self-destruction of all kinds, for he would have gladly blown himself to smithereens for fun, if only it wouldn't have interfered so permanently with his plans.

Etienne was not there the night Jacaranda and Max had gone to a little dinner for six given by the people who were only visiting at a hotel in L.A. (They really couldn't exist anywhere but the center of the Nile, in some place like the George V in Paris or the clean sands of Rio.) That night Jacaranda had become officially "Impossible." She had turned twenty-eight.

She had been sitting in her apartment looking at Emilio, and at a crate weighing sixty pounds that had just been delivered from Vendome, a fancy liquor store; a wooden crate covered with mint silver paper, tied with a pink bow, containing a case of French wine (thirty-seven dollars a bottle—she telephoned to find out—and *she* was broke). The card said "Etienne."

What happened, she never really knew in exact detail. But Jacaranda managed to sin; in the movies, unforgivable acts were usually called "sins." She knew that she came in and they were serving some cocktail called a White Lady, made out of vodka and cream and some liqueur, and she had about fourteen of them.

Fourteen White Ladies made her begin to think that she was doomed. So many of the ones like her, the ones who were brought aboard to amuse the barge, disappeared. They O.D.'d on Quaaludes and Tuinals or got hepatitis and had to retire forever, or they became like Marianne, a zombie girl she'd known, who would drop her purse in public and have to spend an hour finding the things and putting them back in—Marianne who was an out-and-out junkie, an old-time heroin dope fiend like Charlie Parker or "the man with the golden arm." There seemed no place to go, after fourteen White Ladies, but into a spin that fell out of the sky, a smashed victim of impending gravity.

But no wonder, she thought, on about her twelfth White Lady, they all sank from sight from the barge. It was all so Impossible; not just her—everything. It was always the same, every town and every bite of food, everything was always permanently the same. Max didn't care anymore.

They talked about the newest places to eat and the newest places to become slender. They talked about the very newest people, and then talked about the very most fabulous oldest people. They talked about how "boring" anyone was who behaved with the least bit less surface élan than Cole Porter. Anyone who was serious about something other than what color to do the hall was boring. Anyone who became as Impossible as Jacaranda was simply too boring and would probably end up doing something truly boring like crashing into a telephone pole or weighing two hundred and twenty pounds.

By the fourteenth White Lady, Jacaranda saw clearly how Impossible it all was. Max thought Jacaranda was so boring that he had spent the entire evening—except for the same dinner they always ate everywhere—playing solitaire, his back toward her.

And so she got on her high horse, told them all that *she* was leaving and that "this town isn't big enough for both of us." She told them all, including Max—especially Max —that she didn't care, that it was always the same, every night, the same! And she jumped off the barge into the crocodile-loaded river and washed ashore, somehow, the following day—in one piece, two arms, two legs—not even a finger missing. She was lucky. Not just about the crocodiles and being in one piece, but because most of the girls they used for local color died before they were thirty.

WHAT JACARANDA HAD done to jump off the barge that dangerous night, to drive out into the streets on fourteen White Ladies, on vodka and vodka and vodka, only white and opaque, instead of being driven home or made to lie down, instead of being looked after the way they usually did for her when she became too Impossible, had been to commit a sin. Aboard the barge there were a few things you could commit which earned the title "sin." Fucking children, shooting anything up, killing someone, killing someone and not remembering, butchering property or animals or love, being lobotomized, stealing, wrecking art, committing suicide or enjoining someone to commit suicide, giving some rare case of V.D. to "every one" of the "dear friends" in the entire world's linkup, blowing up a church, selling arms to heinous monsters, burning down a National Park— none of these things could be seriously considered by those aboard the barge as a sin; "unfortunate timing" perhaps, or, at worst, "a deplorable misjudgment," but "sin? My dear, what shall you have to drink? Are you going to Castelli for the opening? I can't decide what to wear, can you?"

SHE COULD NEVER really explain about the solitaire or the White Ladies to anyone. And what had happened on the pier that time with Max—a perfectly vile example of Max's behavior—was so ordinary, she hated to have to fall back on it, when, later, she tried to explain what was wrong with Max.

The Pier

People whose understanding of Max came from seeing him at an occasional party or from hearing Jacaranda talk about him could not imagine later on why she came to think of him as such a threat.

"But what—exactly—did he *do?*" they'd ask.

"But I *told* you," she'd reply. "He'd say things that made me hide under the covers for two days."

"What *kind* of things?" they'd ask.

"I told you," she'd say. "He called up the day after some Etienne party and said, 'Why were you so mean to Lydia?'"

". . . Oh," they'd say.

"Let me tell you about the pier, then," Jacaranda suggested one day to a friend who didn't comprehend.

IT MUST HAVE been the third or fourth year, the third, that Jacaranda had known Max. At that time she had come to regard him as somewhat of a conscience. His ability to send her under the covers for two days had already been unsheathed.

One night the phone rang.

Jacaranda was home on mescaline with a friend who wasn't, a man who was too well-meaning and sincere to keep her from yawning and drinking tequila by the large gulpful. She was so happy that the phone had rung.

"Hello?" she said.

"You're *here!*" he said.

"Well, *I'm* here," she said. "Where are you? L.A.?"

"Gilbert and Tom and I are just down the beach from you. What are you doing?" he drawled.

"I'll be right there," she said.

She managed to remember to take her purse and made her sincere friend drop her off at Tom's studio.

Tom's studio was in a condemned ex-restaurant on a pier that was also condemned, in a neighborhood that was about to be rolled into dust and rebuilt with large dwellings suitable for stewardesses and singles.

Jacaranda let herself in. It was bleak and terrifying, and dark red splashes were all over the floors. Tom's latest girl lay asleep in a hammock, candles cast Poe-like reflections, and the drink that night was Bloody Marys with lots of Tabasco sauce. Max and Gilbert and Tom-the-artist were slouched in a small circle on the pillowed floor in a corner.

"We're all on LSD," Max announced.

"Perfect," Jacaranda said, looking around and smelling piers, old piers about to crumble, made of dried-out wood, with mussels clinging to the underwater posts and artists squatting higher up. "I'm out of my mind, too," she said. "What are you drinking?"

The four of them, never waking the sleeping girl in the hammock above, stayed up all night in a game of mixed doubles. Around Max there was always competition, even when he was playing Who Can Be the Most Modest and Humble. Jacaranda figured that if Max ganged up on her too much, she'd have Tom there to scare Max off. Tom was one of the only artists in L.A. who had immediately regarded Max as a crafty hustler and had told Max so. Max began spending every waking moment concocting irresistible little transcendent specialties for Tom. Max even abandoned Etienne for a few months in order to unravel the secrets of the pier. However, Jacaranda never thought that Tom, who rode around in his truck with a sawed-off shotgun and who for a whole month had lived out in the desert all by himself with only a knife—Tom, whose art was bleak and translucent and inaccessible—would abandon an old surfing companion like her for Max's white ironed and folded cloth napkins. But he did.

Max began to turn the night into a game of Get Jacaranda. He brought up everything she'd ever done, each attack the least bit embellished. Tom joined in moving the date of things Jacaranda was guilty of to when she was in junior high.

"Tom," Jacaranda said, "you've sold out."

"What do you mean?" Max asked.

"What's he given you?" Jacaranda asked Tom, nodding her head in Max's direction.

"Me? What have *I* given him?" Max asked.

"Nothing," Tom said, looking down.

"Liar," Jacaranda said.

"Max is fixing it so Tom can have a show in Rome this fall," Gilbert blandly announced.

Gilbert had been leaning against his dark cushion in the circle, completely silent until that moment. Gilbert's ashy eyes looked up and around now. Max had suddenly disappeared. Tom went to the kitchen to make more Bloody Marys.

"How are you?" Jacaranda asked Gilbert.

"Look, I don't really see Max anymore," Gilbert said. "He's too dangerous. He likes to get close to us, and for a while he gets a rush off our edge but in the meantime he's asking so many questions and talking so much that he softens us up. Once that happens, he doesn't care anymore and goes on to the next one."

"Did he do that to you?" Jacaranda asked.

"I thought Max was just some harmless queen with a weird sense of humor . . . Anyway, I just ran into him and Tom at some party and I thought what the hell. Do you know Tom's got a trunkful of grenades? For when the C.I.A. discovers the real meaning of those awful pieces he does?"

Max and Tom appeared wheeling two old bicycles.

"We're going out," Tom said.

"It's pitch dark," Jacaranda said.

"No, it's not; it's dawn," Max said.

Jacaranda looked at a window above. It was gray outside.

Tom and Max went out the front door and it slammed.

As the room began to lighten, Jacaranda felt her mescaline glee begin to crumble away. She and Gilbert decided to make some civilized coffee. When they returned to the room, it was no longer a robbers' den where assassination plots were being hatched; it was the Morning After, when the candles are burnt down to the end and cigarette butts and old Bloody Marys are all that remain.

Gilbert had just agreed to drive Jacaranda home after they finished their coffee when the door opened and Max and Tom rollicked in.

They brought the foggy dawn with them and they panted from their morning exercise. Max stood there in his jeans and old blue work shirt, his Bonnie Prince Charlie attitude and his magnetic laughter, with Tom beside him, his brown braid and his brown beard and his brown eyes aglow with health and sophisticated good will. For some reason they struck Jacaranda as Young Men of Fashion out on a Lark. Maybe it was Max's entrance combined with the camaraderie that was now so plain in Tom.

" . . . and we were going along the boardwalk," Max plunged ahead, "sort of lookin' out at the beach—"

"And you know the bums are all out there at 5 a.m. picking up pop bottles to sell for cheap wine," Tom interrupted.

Tom and Max had decided, it would be jolly to dismount, leave their bicycles, and satisfy their curiosity about what it was these bums actually did.

They spied a likely bum and set forth on their expedition and questioned the old man in their eager-young-lord adventure with the lower classes.

A police car, driving by, saw this suspicious-looking group and stopped.

The police questioned Max, Tom, and the bum.

"And when they saw we weren't really doing anything," Tom said, "they were embarrassed, so they took the bum in for creating a disturbance."

"They *what?*" Jacaranda said. "*You* guys just let someone be taken to *jail?*"

"It's O.K.," Max said.

"Yeah," Tom said. "They're used to it. They throw those guys in jail all the time."

"*Used* to it?" Jacaranda fumed.

"Is that coffee?" Max asked. "I'm hungry, let's go eat." Gilbert shot a look at Jacaranda and shrugged. He said, "We're tired. I'm driving Jacaranda home."

Gilbert's profile against the misty morning wasn't half as cruel as it might have been if the mean side had been the side facing her.

TO FRIENDS WHO didn't comprehend Max, Jacaranda seldom recalled the story about the bum. For one thing, she didn't like to be reminded of Max's scientific, detached sparkle. It made her question why human beings always appeared to be coming along so nicely as a whole when the bottom would fall out once again and they began collecting ears and fillings from each other's heads.

Besides, Max's carelessness about the bum wasn't what upset her. People do careless horrible things to each other morning, noon, and night—everyone does—and the story about the bum was simply an isolated moment about which one could get righteously indignant and know whom to be indignant *at* for a change. People go through life eating lamb chops and breaking their mother's hearts.

Jacaranda felt Max was truly dangerous because of her painting. She'd drawn and painted all her life: ladies with whips, bluebirds, clouds in the skies. But then one day Max paused, stood back from one of her surfboards, and said, "Is that the blue you're using?"

After that, she just stopped painting.

Empty Barge Blues

Maybe it was what Gilbert said. Maybe Max, once Jacaranda softened up and wouldn't even risk blue paint anymore, had found bluer pastures, leaving Jacaranda ashore.

Or maybe after fourteen White Ladies Jacaranda abandoned the barge as she thought at the time she did.

On the other hand, it might have been the writing. The writing was probably it. They all urged her to stop. Jacaranda, however, knew they weren't really serious. She only wrote to do something during the day. And it was just a surfing essay, which no one would even have noticed if it hadn't been published.

Jacaranda knew a lot of writers (none on the barge, however, except very, very hollow ones who would never jeopardize their position by giving away the plot). One day, a woman friend of hers who was a famous writer wrote to an editor of a very prestigious magazine and told him about Jacaranda, who'd written this little *tour de force* about learning to surf. Jacaranda sent in the piece. The man sent her a check for $250. The piece was published. It was given the magazine's center-fold spread with lots of white around it. People began calling her, saying, "I didn't know you could write."

That was another sin.

She could get published in a sound journal that meant business and didn't publish fly-by-nights. She was twenty-eight. It was time for her to O.D., not get published.

Etienne, being a man of action, opened the door of his Silver Cloud, sat her down next to him—just the two of them alone—and said: "Don't write."

Max, trying to keep his banner of truth before him, said, "You should write poetry; you have a gifted ear for language. You shouldn't write prose or anything that is all tarted up with 'ideas' and 'facts.'"

The women, one by one, took her into the bedrooms of parties and said, "Don't write, darling. It's not nice."

The purple fire died down in Etienne's eyes but Jacaranda was too drunk to notice.

Again and again, various people from the barge took Jacaranda aside and looked serious as they pleaded with her. But she knew they weren't serious.

Several of the men, the less smart ones, took her out and asked: "Do you mind if I ask a very personal question? How do you write?"

Maybe once she began to write, they regretted that they'd ever allowed her on board the barge in the first place. Of course, they knew that local color is playing with fire but they liked taking risks. Perhaps it was too much that everything they did and said might be recorded by some L.A. native girl who didn't understand very much in the first place.

Maybe it was all of those things.

After the fourteen White Ladies, Max left Los Angeles. Neither he nor any of the barge—even Etienne—ever seemed to come back to L.A. again for any reason. The only one who remembered her was Lydia Antonia. Poorer adventuresses in need of a cheap apartment called Jacaranda saying that Lydia had told them to look her up when they came to L.A.

The Working Girl
(*Xeroxing*)

Jacaranda got a job Xeroxing at a Postal Instant Press branch near Santa Monica. The place was a hotbed of L.A. cultural activity because it was besieged by people who'd written movie scripts, movie treatments, and TV pilot first drafts, as well as actors Xeroxing scenes to rehearse or pages for screen tests.

She loved working there because it was so clean and spacious and red, white, and blue. Everything, from the cardboard boxes and paper bags to the outside of the storefront and the rugs, was red, white, and blue. The counter was blue. Branches of P.I.P. were opening up all over L.A.

Jacaranda continued to write articles.

The magazine editor who published her newer pieces was a true sport. The magazine was only sold in Southern California and was supposed to have been dedicated to L.A.'s cultural events, but the editor let Jacaranda write about whatever she wanted. He paid her what he could afford.

Jacaranda loved coming to work and Xeroxing all those movies that would never be made and TV ideas that would never even be taped, much less canceled.

Jacaranda befriended the people who'd opened a new place near her apartment in Santa Monica called the Bamboo Café. They wound up letting her drink all the white wine she wanted for free because the people who came to the Bamboo Café liked having a published author around, drunk or not.

Jacaranda was making ends meet from the part-time Xeroxing-job salary of seventy-eight dollars a week and the magazine-article money. She figured that any day now she was going to start feeling the simple composure of normalcy that Jane Austen's heroines always sought to maintain, the state described in those days as "countenance," and later as "being cool." But Jacaranda was always losing her countenance and was not in the least cool. Anyone coming into her apartment, where she'd lived for five whole years, would wonder even more, because the living room had no furniture at all in it—just a basketball, one bed, one TV, and forks. She wasn't even good at square uncool virtues like couches or traditional bedspreads. She typed on the rug.

One night two things happened in the Bamboo Café: Shelby Coryell and Janet Wilton.

The Bamboo Café

The Bamboo Café was designed by artists and looked like an L.A.–*Flying Down to Rio* banana-leaf ode. Its walls were pink and its tablecloths were chartreuse like the floor (which was marbled in pink).

Artificial flamingos stood in the front windows among chartreuse banana leaves. And flamingos in chartreuse were silhouetted against the pink wallpaper.

The place sat about seventy people. Most of them were resigned to what they referred to as paying "New York prices" for dinner even though the restaurant was in Ocean Park, right next to Venice, which was certainly not a thing like New York. The food was uneven; it was supposed to be L.A.–Mediterranean.

The waitresses all wore little black elastic tops and tight black pants, and they were all blond and not easily tricked. The busboys were what gay men currently referred to as "twinkies," which meant they were cute enough to eat.

Salvatore, the owner, an Italian Canadian from Montreal, basked in his glory, for the place very quickly became *the* place.

Destiny Takes a Hand

Jacaranda had met Shelby Coryell when they were both fourteen, surfing. She thought he was hers from the moment she saw him rising out of the sea like a Hawaiian coyote, with thick straight black hair and ridiculous bronze eyes. She'd never been especially in love with Shelby; she'd just more or less taken possession of him, from the time they met forever after.

But she'd forgotten about him in large patches; years had gone by since she'd even seen him before that day in the Bamboo Café. She forgot about him completely when she first ran off with Colman and had moved inland. Shelby became what's known as an "L.A. artist"—a master of the finish—a mad fiend for perfection. Now he lived down in Venice, just south of Santa Monica, and, unlike Jacaranda, he was lean and went surfing every morning even though he was almost thirty. And she'd forgotten about Shelby again when she found Gilbert out in the monsoon on North Shore's Sunset Beach. Since then, she hadn't seen Shelby Coryell except once or twice at Max's.

Shelby, the day he came into the Bamboo Café, was still the same, the L.A. artist, tall and slender, the master-of-balance surfer he'd always been, and he still had that edge of elegant old-fashioned good manners. He was wearing faded old jeans and a bleached-out Hawaiian shirt, and all the women in the restaurant stopped, their glasses halfway to their lips, their sentences unfinished—Shelby was more wicked and coyote-looking than ever, more silent and strange, more of a siren song about the islands.

"Sometimes I feel like you're my twin," he told her once, "and every time you say something particularly awful— even when I'm not there—I feel a sharp pain in my groin."

The restaurant was jammed and at its most insane with people four deep at the bar. The Django Reinhardt– Stéphane Grappelli tape was drowned out and the pink-and-chartreuse décor was barely visible in the hubbub. Jacaranda was having dinner with eight people, all of whom let her talk the whole time. But she went outside with Shelby.

"I heard you came here," he said, smiling, "but you're with people. Will you be busy later?"

Jacaranda wrote out her address and phone number and watched him glide away toward his car. How anyone, especially she, could have forgotten an ace in the hole like Shelby was really impossible to understand. He had always been such a peerless creature. Shelby had the manners of a prince (an imaginary one, not a real one; real ones had no manners), the bearing of a noble spirit. She could tell him everything and he never got bored if she didn't stay clever. No lights went out in his eyes.

And he could tell her anything: boring things about what he'd been doing—only she didn't get bored, she just liked the sound of his voice. He knew more about her than any man ever had; he, after all, had been hers from the beginning, the one who was there when she first knew what she liked. And they had laughed together, of course, and had mentioned the names of brothers and cousins and aunts and outlandish principals in each of their lives without having to explain everything, when explaining everything never explained anything about things like that.

JANET WILTON AND her party of three were sitting at the corner table under the banana-leaf water color that the owner of the Bamboo Café thought was bamboo. Nothing was bamboo in the restaurant.

Janet Wilton worked for an entertainment agency, A.I.M., where she was a literary agent in the New York office. She was out on the Coast to crack skulls and let it bleed; she was "the hottest agent in New York," as everyone in New York knew. (Even at P.I.P. in Santa Monica, the ones who really knew the movie business knew who Janet Wilton was and the kind of deals she'd engineered.) Jacaranda didn't get too good a look at Janet until just as she was leaving to go meet Shelby.

"Hello," Janet Wilton said, in a voice flat on the ground from the streets of New York City. "Are you Jacaranda Leven?"

Jacaranda saw a chic impossible rust-colored fashion plate with a cement voice.

"Yes," Jacaranda said, "I'm Jacaranda Leven. What are you?"

"I'm a literary agent from New York City," Janet Wilton said, handing Jacaranda her card. "I've read some of your pieces and I'd like to represent you. Call me collect on Monday. I'll be back in New York by then. Call me on Monday," Janet Wilton repeated as her party stood up, two men in dark suits with ties, and another woman also rust-colored with boots and tweed and all sorts of expensive tasteful soft things that looked blindly misguided out at the beach.

Jacaranda tried to focus on Janet Wilton but all she could remember other than that voice was that the woman was wearing ruby stud earrings.

$1,200

Jacaranda called Janet Wilton collect as Janet had told her to. The following day, Jacaranda mailed an article she'd written that she thought maybe somebody might like to Janet. A week later, Janet telephoned to say it had been accepted by a large magazine and that they were paying $1,200 to publish it.

"They want you to write more for them," Janet explained, "but I told them you'd be busy working on your book and might not have the time."

"Oh," Jacaranda said.

The check came, minus Janet's 10 percent.

Jacaranda quit P.I.P., and from that point only came back when she had to Xerox her own things.

She took Shelby out for dinner and they drank champagne.

When the piece ran in the magazine, Colman, her old boy friend, called her for the first time in six years and congratulated her, his voice confident with soft intimate lies. "Hey, kid, I read your piece in the magazine—pretty good. I always knew you had it in you. Got any dynamite screenplays hanging around?" Colman was a director. He was rich and famous and she could have promised that as soon as she got an idea for a dynamite screenplay she'd call him up instantly and let him rob her blind. Instead she said, "Talk to my agent, Colman, she does all the business stuff. She's Janet Wilton, you know?"

"Janet Wilton's your agent?" he asked, amazement seeping truth into his voice.

"In New York," Jacaranda said.

The Drinking Problem

J acaranda had a drinking problem. It seemed to have crept up on her at about the same time Max did. Not that it was Max's fault, perhaps.

Anyway, writers all had drinking problems in the twentieth century, and once she got the $1,080 check, she was obviously a writer and it was obviously the twentieth century, so of course she had a drinking problem.

She discovered what most writers insist is true nowadays, which is that they can only write for three hours a day at the most, so what else is there to do but drink?

She was, after all, so glad that she'd turned out to be a writer, since if her drinking problem had been what it was and she'd been only a Xerox operator, she might have been tempted to go to A.A.

In fact, she recommended becoming a published author to all people with drinking problems. A writer can blunder through life like Norman Mailer with his "tiny fist" striking out at cocktail parties, and all anyone will think is that he is a classical drunk writer. If he did something like that and worked at P.I.P., one of the musclebound stock boys would break his head.

The Problem With "The Book," Part 1

From the moment Jacaranda was transformed by the magical wand of Janet Wilton's "representation" from a slatternly working girl into a composed woman of letters, there was the problem—at first obvious only to Janet—of "the book."

Every Monday at 7 a.m., Jacaranda's phone would ring. It would be ten o'clock in New York and Janet would be calling. "Hello," she'd say, her voice sinking like a stone anchor into Jacaranda's sleep. "Oh, are you asleep?"

"No, yes . . . maybe," Jacaranda would say. "What do you mean by 'sleep?'"

"I called to tell you that *Vogue* is interested in having you do a piece for them, but I told them that I wasn't having you do anything that might interfere with the book."

"What book?" Jacaranda, for the first month or so, used to ask.

"The book" was a figment of Janet Wilton's imagination. To Janet, this book was something that Jacaranda was working on with a sort of overall thoroughness. To Janet, it was something that needed time to germinate. It was something for which all of New York City, in Janet's opinion, was waiting. "The book" was the serious thing, the thing that—as time began to pass and the Mondays mounted up—Jacaranda at last, through the density of her hangovers and general Los Angeles naïveté, realized was *why* Janet Wilton was "representing" her in the first place.

To become a suitable author for Janet Wilton to represent, Jacaranda *had* to write a book. Being a magazine writer was small potatoes, boondock Kalamazoo-type provincial; it did no good to Janet Wilton to represent a magazine writer who *only* made $1,200 for a piece when Janet could, with the same expenditure of energy, sell an advance on a book for $10,000, and—if the book proved hot—get into the interesting tangle of paperback/movie infinities.

But despite knowing it, Jacaranda invented an artificial bouquet of excuses, which, if gazed upon from across the room, looked as though they'd smell like real flowers—like roses and lilacs and sweet peas—if one got closer. Jacaranda decided that Janet Wilton had taken her and her magazine pieces because of their genius. Jacaranda also decided that Janet Wilton couldn't really be serious about "the book," that she only mentioned it the way some men made passes at women—somewhat like a percentage player covering as many bases as possible. When things got too close and the calls from Janet became too frequent and the flowers began to look awfully fishy, Jacaranda would pick a fight with Shelby and he would make her cry.

"How's the book?" Janet Wilton would inquire.

"Shelby's gone to Laguna without me," Jacaranda would cry.

Whenever someone—herself included—was having a romantic catastrophe, Janet Wilton, despite her incredible sophistication and world-wise demeanor, would fall apart at the seams.

Jacaranda had discovered this sympathetic loophole in Janet Wilton and cried about Shelby whenever Janet began getting too logical about "the book." Janet simply would not have understood what was taking Jacaranda so long, otherwise.

Jacaranda knew that she probably had enough material lying around her apartment for three large books, but she certainly was not about to mail it all to Janet Wilton, who would read it only to realize that Jacaranda was not the sort of author for A.I.M., that it was all an unfortunate silly mistake, and that Jacaranda would understand, and that "there are plenty of other fine agencies these days and I'm sure you'll find one more suitable for your work."

Jacaranda knew plain as day that even if Janet Wilton mistakenly continued to represent her after she sent enough things for "the book" to New York, no publisher would want to publish her. And once Janet Wilton counted the twenty-nine rejections for Jacaranda's "book," she'd be even more irritated for having been taken in by Jacaranda's tawdry glamorizing and cheap tricks.

On the other hand, of course, she knew that the pieces she'd published so far were making an enormous difference in her life and changing everything unmercifully.

Jacaranda had come to feel at home with the idea that she was much too L.A. ever to be taken seriously. Only deadpan architectural historians from England took L.A. seriously, and Jacaranda wished they hadn't, because she liked L.A. the way it was—anonymous. She had come to appreciate anonymity. When her first pieces were published after Janet Wilton became her agent, she couldn't stand to look at them. It seemed to her that the words were all bunched together in straitjacket-width columns, just as her thoughts and stories were. (In the local magazine, the right margins had been open like blank verse, which made it a lot easier for her to bear.) Suddenly she was being read by people she didn't know, and they probably felt the way she did about writers who published in big-time magazines, which was that they had something well thought out and clearly stated to tell her, and that they were professional and glossy and awe-inspiring. And since she hardly ever met any magazine writers whose articles she'd read, she saw no reason to imagine that they might be falling apart just like everyone else, no matter how falling-apart they often wrote they were. They must have begun in life knowing they were going to amount to something, and make money, and have furniture, and be otherwise successful, whereas she had always known she wouldn't.

Along with the notion of going places contentedly as an anonymous Xeroxer, she also had long since accustomed herself to the idea that she would never ever be able to make money. Money was for other people who had some inside system of How Things Work. She was actually terrified of the money that had begun cascading down on top of her (though other people would hardly think it was that much, since executive secretaries, like her friend Wini, made twice as much, and their health was insured on top of it. Jacaranda had once heard that an artist was "any white person over twenty-five without health insurance").

Jacaranda managed to stay fairly broke by paying her father back the quarter of a million dollars she figured she owed him.

But even the slightest taint of "fame" was not comforting. All her life she'd skated along making most people think that she was not really there and would never be able to remember what she saw, or put it together afterward even if she did. But now people who had read her pieces were careful not to leak any secrets that weren't souped up. People would take her aside when she first got to parties to tell her they'd just had an abortion, were writing a screenplay about it, and to ask whom did she think they ought to get to direct.

Jacaranda liked it a lot better when people thought she was Shelby's girlfriend or some fly-by-night art groupie. The more someone liked her writing, the fewer clothes she felt she had on.

Whenever Janet Wilton telephoned at 7 a.m. on Monday to find out how the book was getting along, Jacaranda attempted to trick Janet into being her agent just a little bit longer by refusing to let her see the book and find out it wasn't the book she had in mind.

Shelby Coryell had heard that women were hysterical, and resigned himself to Jacaranda's lifelike accusations that he didn't love her. (She had to *believe* how awful Shelby was when she described him to Janet Wilton or she'd never have been able to sound convincing.)

Shelby would come back from Laguna to find Jacaranda languishing from a broken heart.

"You went to Laguna without me," she'd weep.

"You said you wanted to stay home," he'd reply. "You said you were working on your book."

I must have been drunk, she thought.

"Janet call today or something?" he'd ask, heading for the icebox for a cream fix.

"Yeah, what is this, ESP?"

"She really wants that book, doesn't she?" he always ended up saying on the days when he found Jacaranda in tears with blood in her eye.

"*I* can't write a whole book!" Jacaranda declared. "I *can't!*"

Her drinking problem was in robust condition, while Shelby would get halfway through one can of beer and not even finish it.

The Forty-Seventh Monday

By the forty-seventh Monday morning, Jacaranda knew how "the book" was going to be, what it was going to be called, and how, by snagging like crochet all her little wayward pieces together, she could pull them into one overall book. She was going to do that. But she didn't want to—she couldn't bring herself to—*tell* Janet Wilton until, finally, one morning, to get her off her back, she just mailed it off—title and all, the book. She mailed it on a Saturday, and when Janet called on the Monday, Jacaranda said, "You'll be getting it this week."

"Oh," Janet had said, the stone anchor in her voice actually lifting as though the boat above were finally going to get to go somewhere. ". . . Good!"

"Thank you, Janet," Jacaranda added, the first time she'd ever really meant a thank-you in her life.

"You're welcome," Janet Wilton replied, not opposed to a little grace when it was suggested by circumstance, although grace was not one of Janet Wilton's criteria for life's forward march.

"The Pain" of the book was made up of innocent little garden snakes—money and fame—compared to "the pain" that Jacaranda saw cross other writers' faces. Real pain only crossed Jacaranda's face when she thought about Max. And she tried—she was getting good trying—not to think about Max, ever. After she'd jumped off the barge, she still drank, but was bolstered by Shelby and

Janet Wilton. She only sometimes heard the sound of Max laughing, and that was at night in her dreams. And sometimes, too, when she looked at Shelby, because there was something about Shelby Coryell—something about the way he walked, and about his cheekbones—that was very much like Max. At sunset, against oleanders, Shelby's profile was four golden heartbeats of Proustian recaptured memories, the memory of the moment she fell in love with that slippery Southern *beaux-yeux*, that beautiful-eyed man. And his voice, Shelby's voice, was like Max's, only softer and drawled in an L.A. drawl. And when Jacaranda would drop by his studio unannounced and Shelby would open the door for her, his eyes would clear from the cloudiness they'd fallen into while thinking of his work; his eyes would see her, and his face would light up, he'd smile, and he would cry: "You're *here!*"

The Problem with "The Book." Part 2

The book got accepted. The publishing company, Dobson & Dalloway, which accepted Jacaranda's book was "the best" publishing company in America and they were the first one to be offered "the book."

All the whole year that Janet Wilton had telephoned Jacaranda Monday at 7 a.m. about "the book," Janet had been egged on every Friday at 4 p.m. by a phone call from Wallace Moss, a young editor at Dobson & Dalloway, who was interested in Jacaranda Leven. "I want to see anything she writes that even remotely resembles a book. I don't care what it is." So Janet Wilton sent the huge hodgepodge of loosely pasted-together material over to Wallace Moss and, *voilà*, Wallace Moss, after reading it over the weekend, called Monday morning at ten and said, "We'll pay five thousand dollars as an advance."

"O.K. Six," Janet Wilton agreed.

At 7:10, L.A. time, Janet telephoned Jacaranda to tell her that part one of the advance would be mailed within the month. The rule was that the author got half the advance when the book was accepted and the other half when it was in publishable shape. Jacaranda's book was *not* in publishable shape by any stretch of the imagination.

"You mean they *bought* it?" Jacaranda cried, screaming Shelby awake and making Emilio fly out the window and not come back for two hours even though breakfast was at eight.

"Sure," Janet Wilton said, relaxing her grip for the first time since Jacaranda had known her, sounding as though she were stretching. "They've been crazy for you for a long time. Of course, don't try and pull any fast ones on Wally Moss, because he'll be able to see through you in a minute. I told you you were writing a book. And I was right."

"You did? Tell me, I mean?" Jacaranda asked, because after a liter and a half of white, she never remembered anything except stripped-bare essentials like "Look, here's my card call me collect on Monday."

"Now." Janet sighed, tensing herself for the next major hurdle. "When are you coming to New York?"

This was in March. In March the year before, she'd become Jacaranda's agent.

"New York?" Jacaranda asked, hearing that voice of Janet's leaden up like molten steel hitting freezing water. "*When* am I coming?"

"You ought to come to New York. Meet your editor. Meet magazine editors. Meet people. How will they know who you are if you just stay in Los Angeles all the time? They have to *see* you, *see* who you are . . ." Her voice had returned to its normal heart-of-stone self. "Now, when are you coming?"

"Oh, my God, I think my cat's just been run over!" Jacaranda shrieked, an inspiration. And she hung up.

From then on, Mondays-at-seven phone calls were "Now, when are you . . ."

Jacaranda's excuses grew thinner and thinner and her fights with Shelby Coryell more and more cataclysmic. If she ever really lost Shelby, she'd die, right there— so, assuming that he knew this, she tore into him like a vampire-bat platoon.

Shelby Coryell was long-suffering. After a while, he realized that until Jacaranda went to New York he wasn't going to have a moment's peace. And he began to absent himself more and more.

But Jacaranda couldn't face New York. New York had Max in it. She'd be bound to run smack into him just walking down the street. What was so great about L.A. was that you never ever ran into anyone by accident, only purposely. Nobody was "at large" on the streets; there were too many streets, and people were either inside their cars or home. But in New York, Max was everywhere. He was on Fifth Avenue, Park Avenue, in restaurant lobbies, coming out of taxis, waiting inside of elevators, going into fancy grocery stores, eating a hot dog on the escalator of the Pan Am Building, shouting across the street at her from a limousine all abloom with feather-boaed summer-barge princesses. And Max, in white, with that laugh. She just couldn't go to New York.

Etienne had a suite at the Pierre Hotel, a place Jacaranda in her imagination saw as resplendent with brocaded satin couches and decanters of sherry and wall safes.

Jacaranda had heard that Max always refused to stay at the Pierre when he was in New York. He called it "a hotel for old ladies" and insisted on staying in a small one-room ex-maid's-quarters ninth-floor apartment at the Dakota, where he lived—it was rumored—like a monk with a mattress on the floor and no record player. When Max was at the Dakota, he only ate brown rice and celery.

New York struck her as impossible for another reason. Jacaranda was afraid of New York—all alone by herself, with no ocean (the Atlantic was not an ocean). She'd heard from infancy that South Carolina was just about the only place on that East Coast where you could surf, and if you couldn't surf on an ocean, it wasn't the ocean. She'd be all alone with no ocean, no surf, and she would run smack into Max . . . She just *couldn't* go to New York. And she was terrified of going someplace and being drunk all the time.

If people like Janet Wilton and Wallace Moss saw her on her third liter of white wine, they were bound to notice and get suspicious and start wondering. She might be able to convince them that she'd simply gone overboard owing to jet lag and provincialism, but then what if she got just as blasted the very next day at, say, around eleven in the morning? What if she went around drunk to see all the people Janet Wilton wanted her to meet at those magazines, where all they knew about Jacaranda was that they published her, not that she was likely to black out before dessert?

New York was so public. Everyone would look at her and know.

What if she went somewhere like Elaine's and launched into some fourteen–White Lady speech about how all New York critics were rusty old remnants from the Industrial Revolution just like New York itself? They might take it personally.

Besides, New York had weather. What if it started raining and she got all wet or snowy and she froze? She just *couldn't* go to New York.

Shelby would go away for days; he'd skip town and go to Laguna to surf. Jacaranda grew green with anguish from missing him, twisted with glimmers of how she'd die if he really left her.

And every Monday at 7 a.m., Janet Wilton called and asked, "Now, when are you coming to New York?"

Jacaranda had known all along she should never have given in and written that damn book of Janet's. *Now* look at life, she wept, and thought about poking her eyes out. She was always drunk.

The Third of July
(Unbidden Aside)

Jacaranda, by July, had so devastated all she had in the way of the present that any possibilities of her having a future looked remote indeed. In June, she had gotten drunk at a party and screamed at Shelby and forced him out of the state flying on the wings of an angel, flying away to Maui where he had friends with no phone who'd hide him, where the fury of Jacaranda's drunken wrath could not reach him. Nearly all of her friends were afraid of her except the ones who drank as much as she did.

The morning after, they all made those tentative 11:30 phone calls of shameful excuses to each other—beginning with "Did I leave my address book at your place?"—to see if they were still speaking to each other after the unspeakable things they'd said and done the night before. If the reply was as if nothing had happened, then life could go on. And it did with Jacaranda, so that by July her only friends were those who could be counted on to forget their address books.

It was amazing that during this time Jacaranda didn't make any lifelong enemies. She would go to the Bamboo Café every night and ask movie producers, "Are you really casting Cher as Medea?"

Or to her artist friends she'd say, "Kurt Schwitters already did that. Twice."

It was even more amazing that people whom she insulted, and apologized to the next day, whom she insulted again that very evening, were the people who afterward said, "I never knew you drank. Were you really drunk that whole time?" Years and years and years were pocked with holes of things Jacaranda simply didn't remember, with people Jacaranda didn't remember meeting, conversations she didn't remember having, promises and parties and great ideas and projects Jacaranda didn't remember hurling herself into. Mostly, she forgot entirely or else, hurling along, she accidentally found herself in the approximately right spot at the approximately right time, and people mistakenly assumed she was reliable or too early or had written the wrong address or the wrong day.

The years, as far as Jacaranda were concerned, from the time she met Max when she was twenty-three until she jumped off the barge when she was twenty-eight were tilted jello salad. They shimmered if you prodded them.

And toward the end, the last two years, they grew murky because all the canned fruit had—from the natural law of gravity—gravitated toward the drunkest end, the end that was deepest in liquid. The first three years, before she'd written that piece and it was published, shimmered like glorious turquoise-blue postcard-sky jello—like a memory Jacaranda had of the Salton Sea, which she'd seen when she was little. She remembered that there was a petrified ocean, an ocean that was caught inland while the rest of the ocean departed. You could see down to the bottom, so far, absolutely clear turquoise, all the sea life that belonged in the ocean—starfish, sea anemone—things that didn't belong in an inland body of water, a lake, which usually had trout or salmon. But the Salton Sea was absolutely clear and absolutely pure and absolutely ancient. Jacaranda had heard that in the Caribbean you could see down forty or fifty feet to the bottom. The Salton Sea didn't move unless you touched it; it was unbidden by the moon, it had no tides, it lay there in perfect beauty, perfect stillness, out in the middle of the desert. The Salton Sea had been like a barge of the ocean floating atop the sandy desert. And those years—pickled in vodka and white wine and money and Rolls-Royce limousines and the soft clear white *ease* of the barge, the informality and the private comforts—had all been hosted by that drawl, shimmery and turquoise and eternally surprised "You're *here!*"

By the time Jacaranda jumped off the barge, she had an

allergic reaction to alcohol. She needed only one drink to be five drinks drunk and she always had that one drink. She always got five drinks drunk and—five drinks drunk—she drank until she blacked out.

Not a soul except April noticed how much she drank. Or that she was an alcoholic, with all the symptoms they ask you about on the TV questionnaires: 1. Does alcohol intrude on your private life? 2. Does alcohol intrude on your professional life? Up to number 10: Do you sometimes have to have a drink in the morning? Jacaranda could with forthright sincerity staunchly say yes to all ten—and nobody she knew noticed, except April.

"If mother knew how much you drank, she'd die," April said. "That's why I'm not going to tell her. She had enough trouble going to sleep thinking about you and that Max person."

But after Max, Jacaranda got worse, not better. Shelby didn't drink and didn't know how drunk she was getting.

So dangerously did Jacaranda flirt with illusions that she had nearly lost the way back entirely by the eve of the Fourth of July. By that night, she had forgotten that she was only fighting with Shelby so she wouldn't have to go to New York—to get off the hook from Janet Wilton with a sincere-sounding tearful "catastrophe" excuse. By that night, she was deep into a Black Forest like Hansel and Gretel, her trail of bread crumbs being eaten by drinks.

•

"ALL YOU HAVE to do is go to New York for a week or ten days," Shelby complained. "You should go, darling. They want you to. Besides, you'll have such a wonderful time. Gee, I wish I could go."

"Why don't you?" Jacaranda brightened.

"The show," Shelby said. "You know I have to stay here and keep an eye on things." (He was having an exhibit in Pasadena.)

"You never loved me," Jacaranda declared.

"Why don't you just go?" Shelby said, kissing her goodbye.

Shelby left for his studio.

Jacaranda knew Shelby didn't love her and she decided to pay him back. She poured herself a nice double of tequila and her rage grew. She would show him how she dealt with sniveling coyotes who thought they could toy with her affections, tell her they loved her, and then think everything was so simple and all she had to do was go to New York!

She imagined a costume spectacular involving thousands of extras, true romance, heroic victory, and the triumph of good over evil! In her version, the slaves were to burst free of their chains and explode from the catacombs beneath the Colosseum, wielding sabers, killing the wicked decadent Romans, and bring to civilization that simplicity and naturalness of pure reason that, for so long now, it had lacked.

It got to the point that her amateur theatricals took on lifelike semblance; the noise was deafening. She could almost dissolve Janet Wilton's 7 a.m. phone calls and get them to fade out and blend into the movie extras dressed in loincloths all the way back by the pyramids, far from the main action. You couldn't even hear "Now, when are you coming to New York?" amid the roars of Jacaranda's lions and tigers, the rattle of the chains, the surging excitement of the mob in the stands.

Anyway, she couldn't go to New York; she was too fat. Maybe if she got polio and had to go live in an iron lung . . . Max would want to know what she was doing, he'd make her show him her book; he'd apologize later by saying he'd tried to read it, but he gave up because he knew she was so much better or it wasn't his type of thing.

"Oh," he'd drawl to his friends later, "that's just some girl I once knew. She used to be rather charming. But now she just sits around writing prose. You know. Subjects and predicates?"

Not Going to New York

It made Jacaranda angry that Shelby encouraged her to go to New York when she knew she would only drink herself into an earlier grave there and probably be pushed out of a ninety-fourth-story window by Max. She didn't tell him about drinking but she mentioned Max.

"But Max is your friend," Shelby said. "He loves you. Besides"—he sighed, afloat on lyrics from Rogers and Hart —"New York!"

(See? she thought. All men are snakes!)

She conceived of an airtight scheme to pay Shelby back for thinking she ought to go to New York.

The airtight scheme was based on the premise that Shelby Coryell believed religiously in having a good time, especially when you were supposed to, like in New York or at parties. Shelby wanted people to have a good time much more than he cared about her, Jacaranda decided. What she must do is arrange for everyone at the next party to have a horrible time.

The next party was to be on July 3rd, and luckily Jack Ripler was throwing it.

JACK RIPLER WAS ready to bolt just knowing he was having a party, in the first place. Shelby had talked him into it, and on the day of the party Jack insisted that Shelby be there all day to help, because Jack was positive he couldn't have a party and that nobody would come, or that all of L.A. would come and steal his acrylic spray-paint guns and that there wouldn't be enough food and that the police would bust the place.

Jack Ripler was a simple artist who lived in Santa Monica and broke hearts as if there were no tomorrow. But he was comfortable breaking hearts; it was a situation he understood. Whereas this party—!

Jacaranda despised Jack Ripler because of his chin. She'd hated his chin from the first moment she'd laid eyes on him when they were in high school, when he was going around being morose, and "interesting," because he was an artist and *so* sensitive. All his art—he made iron sculpture—jutted out just like his chin. Women thought he was a genius and waited in line to have their hearts broken.

Jack Ripler was what people meant by the word "Scorpio."

She had no idea whether he actually *was* a Scorpio *per se*, but he was intense and unblinking and insinuating. (Jacaranda had grown up hearing her father refer to all ignorant superstition of any kind as the opiate of the masses, but if she was really to live in L.A., she had to know what being a Scorpio meant. Usually she liked Scorpios.)

It seemed like a sensible idea at the time to wreck Jack Ripler's party and thus depress Shelby, and to wreck it in a brilliant, artful way.

Meanwhile

66 "T he book" was sold to Dobson & Dalloway in March and it was that March, the following week, when Janet began badgering Jacaranda to come to New York. Things moved along every Monday as before.

This Wallace Moss, Jacaranda's editor, had telephoned her and said congratulations. He told her how honored he was to be able to work with her and that of course there would have to be major changes, which he'd begin at once.

His voice was icy but cordial, a combination Jacaranda had never remembered hearing. It was sort of like Montgomery Clift trying to be mean.

By May, half the stories had been returned with a cordial note telling her, "We won't be needing these, thank you." Signed "W."

By June, about two-thirds of what was left after the half had been removed was craftily Scotch-taped onto regulation 8 ½" x 11" pages: diabolically, this man Wallace had turned what was once a Jacaranda Leven harum-scarum mess (she was *such* a mess) into an elegant, readable, calmly ordered cloistered hallway. You could practically hear the silence of the silk and satin cloak hems dragging along the cool marble. What had once been harum-scarum was now amazingly graced. It was a book.

By the end of June, Jacaranda received unbound galleys (as opposed to bound galleys, which were to come later and which were to be sent to book reviewers). An unbound Xeroxed copy of how the book would look printed once the errors were proofread out—a "loose proof."

Jacaranda read the loose proof and felt the hair on the back of her neck sharpen with awe. How anyone could— by sheer brilliance and instinct—know that *that* was what she had meant!

But then her obsession about New York overcame her and for a moment, drunkenly, she even thought that Dobson & Dalloway and the book had somehow been in cahoots with New York—with Max—to try and make her forget what a snake Shelby was, and she thought again how great it was going to be to wreck Jack Ripler's party.

Only, drunk as she got, she could never really believe Shelby would be in cahoots with Wallace Moss. Shelby could hardly bear to read at all.

With great effort, she dragged her attention away from the book, and turned her face to where duty lay: right past the Pieta, into the ordinary Vatican junk.

The Plot Lumps Up

Her confusing airtight scheme depended on Sunrise.

Everybody knew that Jack Ripler had had one unsuccessful romance. Just one love affair where in the end what was broken was not the woman's heart. After Jack Ripler recovered, he never was quite as good at pulling off the doomed-genius ennui that had so captivated artists' molls, and rich patrons with husbands and three children.

But everybody had not known everything.

Only Shelby had really known about Sunrise Honey in detail, and of course Shelby always told Jacaranda everything.

Sunrise Honey was a legendary groupie who vanished from rock-'n'-roll when she was still a teen-ager, to move in with Zack Birnbaum, a dope dealer who lived in Laurel Canyon. Zack wore velvet suits and his hair long, but he was basically a man who wanted three meals a day, all cooked, and no dirty dishes afterward. Sunrise Honey felt just like a normal American bride, safe. The least she could do was scramble eggs and wash plates.

Now and then, Zack the dope dealer kicked Sunrise out into L.A.

It was during one of these times that Jack Ripler discovered her and made her come to Topanga and be gorgeous right in his own studio, twenty-four hours a day.

Jacaranda heard that Sunrise Honey never spoke. Everyone was convinced she was retarded.

One night, when Jack Ripler and Sunrise Honey were driving down Topanga in his van, Jack got so angry that he hit Sunrise Honey right across the face. She swerved the car into the bushes, jumped out, opened his door, yanked him upright, and then kicked in three of his ribs.

"*Retarded!*" Jacaranda had laughed, clapping her hands with delight. "She's the smartest girlfriend he's ever had!"

Sunrise Honey disappeared back up into Laurel Canyon. Zack the dope dealer had three meals a day once more, and Jack Ripler went into a depression that convinced even Jacaranda about black holes in space.

"Too bad he's cried wolf for so long," Jacaranda said. "People could feel heartfelt sympathy for him instead of just dried-up old sympathy."

"Poor Jack." Shelby sighed, his sympathy all dried up, too.

When Jack Ripler returned from his morose travels to take his mind off his depression, Shelby was told never to mention Sunrise Honey's name for as long as he lived. Jack moved to Venice. So Jacaranda invited Sunrise Honey to Jack Ripler's party. All she had to do was call Zack Birnbaum and invite him, without saying whose party it was.

Not too many people knew that Zack Birnbaum had taken violin lessons from Mort Leven until he was twelve. He and Jacaranda used to play chess all the time until he learned the phrase "castrating bitch" and insisted that was what any girl was called who beat a guy at chess all the time and never acted feminine, like a normal person of her sex, by letting the man win every so often.

When "castrating bitch" fell into disuse like "nymphomaniac," Zack Birnbaum brought himself up to date and decided that Jacaranda was actually brilliant and "not like most women—silly."

Zack and Jacaranda always meant to "meet for lunch or a drink soon," but it was never this week, and "next week for sure" didn't work out.

Zack was not at all suspicious when Jacaranda invited him to a party. Perhaps he thought that he and Jacaranda were regular old friends. In Jacaranda's mind, when she telephoned, people who got in her way ought to watch out, and it was their own fault if they didn't notice that her voice timbre was that of a dangerous lunatic.

"Oh, and bring Sunrise," Jacaranda said. "I've heard so much about her."

"Really?" Zack said.

"I want to see what she looks like," Jacaranda said.

"She's old," Zack said. "Seven years ago she had something, but now . . . If you're sure, I'll bring her."

"Oh, bring her," Jacaranda said.

WHEN JACARANDA FELL back in love with Shelby, and doubts about the book disappeared, she called Zack and tried to change things, but it was too late.

The Night Was Young

T he night was young and the moon was lopsided.

Sunrise and Zack arrived at Jacaranda's house all dressed and fresh to go to a party.

Jacaranda decided that Sunrise was so beautiful that nothing could hurt her. She was not like other people—all mortal and nose-blowy. Sunrise hardly said hello; she just breathed life into her encasement. Maybe that took all the strength one had, breathing life into what Sunrise looked like.

Sunrise was wearing a white lace wedding dress from the Fourth of July in 1918, when "our boys" came back from gay Paree; a dress that would *keep* them down on the farm (she wasn't wearing a stitch of underwear). The dress was white eyelet, its little lacy holes neatly handsewn throughout the entire faded bridal gown. She wore nothing on her feet. They were flat on the ground. So she looked like a missionary's bastard daughter dressed in hand-me-down pagan-baby donation clothes. She wore no make-up. Sunrise and Zack and Jacaranda drank a toast to the night and Sunrise uttered her first words aloud, in Jacaranda's recollection: "To the third of July."

She looked as if she were about to lift off the ground she was so light, and this, combined with her color, made the name Sunrise Honey seem perfectly sensible. Her skin was honey and the rest of her was sunrise. It rose across a China sea, an Irish sailor adventuring to far-off islands, spices and silks and the pearls of the Orient, the cricket cage, and the tea plantations. The sun rose in the East and the East was the Orient, the destination of Marco Polo, who returned with pasta, oranges, and firecrackers.

Frowning or thinking of something else, Sunrise, motionless, could be mistaken for a madman's broken dream of an Etruscan beauty changed from her normal position on the coffin (lying beside her husband) to sitting in a contemporary setting or flung across a bed.

Jacaranda's beauty had long ago sunk into the sludge of gray-green no-sun pallor; the look—with broken pink-eyed blood veins—of someone "who drinks." She wore simple white pants and a blue flowered top, with a red rose pinned to her bosom—and red-blood toenails. She was a patriot.

Zack, with his evil black hair, his evil black mustache, and his evil black eyes, wore an evil midnight-blue suit made of velvet to go with the lopsided moon. Outside of

L.A. and Rome, innocent bystanders would have believed Zack and Sunrise were about to go onstage in some nearby, if invisible, theater.

Coming out into the night with them, Jacaranda felt fine. Everything would be all right, even if she never got to New York at all.

"Isn't life wonderful?" she asked as they all stepped outside. "Look at the moon!"

Shelby

Jacaranda had fallen into the habit, when in love, of playing mean tricks. She had learned it from Max. Colman had only softened things by his lies, telling her, "Everything's fine with me, darling, peace and quiet, peace and quiet—same old thing, you know me . . ." But Max had seduced her into wanton tangles of breakfast arguments and reckless ease—luxurious evils that ordinary mortals cannot sustain.

Shelby knew that Jacaranda loved him, and he'd always loved her. She knew all about his childhood. But about Max all Jacaranda could really reveal was "He had a way with words."

Jacaranda never could determine if Shelby was dumb or smart. If someone had asked her whether April was dumb or smart, Jacaranda wouldn't have known what to say either. But there was no question about Max: he was smart.

She couldn't believe that there were some experiences in life one cannot afford. The idea that something was beyond one's means was preposterous—other cities had winters, cockroaches, and famine. Not L.A. Henry James, of course, would have known instantly what it was. He'd have diagnosed it without a moment's hesitation: it was European decadence versus New World boldness. In *Daisy Miller*, New World boldness was nipped in the bud—one trip to the Colosseum by moonlight, an adventure only an American girl could conceivably attempt because Europeans knew one would contract Roman fever and die. Boldly, Daisy contracted Roman fever and died. The European decadence made short work of the poor American girl. Henry James would have known that through a series of unlikelihoods Jacaranda would survive. And yet Jacaranda had contracted at least one disease that was fairly terminal: alcoholism. Perhaps it would just take her a little longer to die than Daisy Miller, who was so swiftly cut down by her innocence and bravado and Rome.

The difference here was that Jacaranda was in her own flat city. They were playing on her turf. All gamblers who win basically understand that "controlling the environment" is what matters in games of "chance," like life.

From sources, Jacaranda learned that Max was oiling up New York by telling "everyone" (the barge people) how fat "poor Jacaranda is and how she drinks all the time now, I guess, I don't know. We never see her. Such a shame. Someone said she was waitressing . . ."

Jacaranda had managed to hang on to a scrap of life, though her situation, by July, was hopeless, life or no. Over the years it's been said by people with serious voices: "It's always darkest before the dawn." The dawn is a word meaning sunrise. Not that she ever deserved to see another daybreak.

She glowed proudly as she parked the car and she and Zack and Sunrise walked into the party.

The Foolproof *Tableau Vivant* Meets the Iceberg

They arrived at the party just as it was cresting over the edge. If they'd arrived ten minutes earlier, Jacaranda might have had her moment; Jack Ripler might have drawn back in shock and might have run somewhere to lock himself in. Shelby might have suffered vicarious torment. Ten minutes earlier and Jacaranda could have taken credit for the way the party had pitched forward into utter cataclysmic squalor and nobody would have been the wiser. But by the time they arrived, the party had already collided with the iceberg, the ship's engines were already flooded with drowning sea water, the boat was already lopsided against the flat ocean's horizon.

Jack Ripler had hired a Pinkerton private detective to stand guard at the door and make sure that no one who was not on the twenty-page non-alphabetical-order list could get in. Inside it was almost worse.

Jacaranda, Zack, and Sunrise got in because Sunrise looked at the Pinkerton. And smiled.

Most of the people at Jack Ripler's party were like Jacaranda and Shelby and Zack and Jack Ripler—rabidly ambitious and white. Most of them were linked up with visual images. They were commercial photographers, artists, art directors, and rock-'n'-rollers. Fashion was rampant, L.A. fashion at its peak of tomorrowness. Everyone looked healthy and lithe and contemptuous of trends and popular obsessions. Just about all of them wore clothes from thrift shops, shops they'd sacked from Marin County to Redondo Beach. They wore thrift-shop watches, thrift-shop belt buckles, and thrift-shop shoes. They had on white pants and faded Hawaiian shirts and no shoes or just sandals. They looked as though they had dressed at the last minute and remembered to button at least one button on their way out the door. Only the people who knew that New York was where they did things right, wore pants with creases in them and socks, and were peeling from too much sun all at once on winter skin. People from New York couldn't believe you could call something a party and not have Scotch, just white wine with ice cubes in it.

There were no animals, other than humans, at this party.

Most of the people were in some way, at some time, in the thick of the movie industry and visually pictured adult success as getting to make the kind of movies they wanted and buying real estate with the enormous money they made.

Jacaranda took a familiar look at this party and felt right at home. Sunrise, towering over most people, took a deep breath and gazed around her, her bare feet flat on the cool cement of the studio floor.

There were about two hundred people there, and Jacaranda knew that Sunrise had never been to this studio of Jack's before. Part of Shelby's insistence that Jack Ripler have the July 3rd party was as a studio-warming, though it seemed much more likely to scald and burn from sex and rage instead.

The funny thing was, Jack never even saw Sunrise that night.

Paradise Kisses and Smacks from Hell

"Hello, darling," Shelby whispered, coming up from behind Jacaranda, his arm around her waist, that virgin-spring gurgle in his voice. "You're *here!*"

He swept her around and kissed her.

Their lips softened against each other's, her flesh met his, while her brain was seething with almost forgotten pent-up rage; her flesh was behaving as though Shelby's flesh were her own true love, rescued from a honeymoon near-death accident. She lost consciousness, her flesh swept off into that blue lagoon, silent with palm trees—just she and Shelby marooned and their own private, eternally secure island, which had never been trodden upon by previous tenants and would never grant a newcomer the privilege of its solace.

What was going on between Shelby and Jacaranda must be what is meant by "love." She'd read about love and heard about how people loved each other even when they got old and weren't pretty anymore. Jacaranda could never imagine it; she thought it was for people with something extra inside them, or something less—she never knew it was for *her*. Only suddenly, driving down the street one day, she knew that if Shelby was ever to go away, or die, she would never be the same. She and Shelby kissed; she felt them swimming at their leisure in a lagoon safe from the ocean but *in* and *part* of the ocean. Safe from dry land.

"Darling." He broke away, standing back to take a look at her. "You are so beautiful! I've never seen you in that blue. And the rose! It's just right. God, I love you."

"Oh," Jacaranda said.

"Listen," Shelby said, "promise me you'll stay till the end. We'll go to your place together, O.K.?"

"Uh," Jacaranda said, still limp from the flesh.

Shelby unwound her from his arm and slithered into the crowd, leaving her standing there, a kiss torn in half.

Without Shelby to kiss her, the whole world tilted perilously against romance. Everywhere she looked in this tangle, she saw women who looked sad and men who looked mean. Jacaranda hacked her way to the wine. She found a place where she could wait out the calamity, a hidden-in-the-shadows stair-step where she could sit, slightly above the others, and see everything and not be seen, or stepped on.

The music had probably been engineered by Jack Ripler, because it blasted out of rented stereo loudspeakers, boiling molasses pouring over naked eardrums. It was black and hot while the guests were white and fashionably asexual.

Jacaranda had this sudden hilarious ambition to make a million dollars so she could rent a house with a garden and send out invitations to a formal tea and *have* one. She would have croquet set up out in the garden, and a long table with English tea on one end and China tea on the other. And little cookies in between.

She could feel the rancid tension in the air beneath the lopsided yellow moon's malevolent regard. She could feel some kind of hazy snap, some uproar, about to happen. In Los Angeles it's called "earthquake weather," but Jacaranda knew earthquakes were just a metaphor for any out-of-control slant suddenly tilting beneath your feet. It was tilting violently against romance already, and now she knew that it wasn't just *her* romance.

This would have been the perfect night for a loud crack or a gunshot to go off.

And there was a loud crack.

It was so loud you could hear it above the horrible music: it wasn't the sound, thank God, of gunpowder from a pistol (or a firecracker); it was more the sound of flesh smacking flesh.

A hushed musical gasp rose up from the people beneath the clash of the Temptations' stereoed desires.

There was another loud crack.

The hush grew more intense, the record noise above more obscene.

A circle backed away from a body, which lay, bloodied on white, sprawling, fallen.

Jacaranda stood on a step. She saw the body sprawling on the cement patio. A man standing above, with blood on his hand, was ready to strike again. The body did not attempt to rise and provoke the man.

Then from the man, a voice somehow in harmony with the midnight-blue velvet of his suit, a hiss narrow enough to trickle through the sound and reach even Jacaranda's ears: "I told you not to dance, you bitch. I told you *before.*"

Then the man, seeing that the body was going to stay on the cement, whirled on his heels. People backed away in every direction. The man walked straight to the front gate and was out, past the Pinkerton.

Sunrise was sprawling on the cement and it was Jacaranda's fault.

It was *all* Jacaranda's fault.

Red & White

Jacaranda could see Sunrise was breathing. So delicately was she assembled that her gasps for breath looked like a magnified insect in slow motion.

Jacaranda sat down next to Sunrise just as she was coming into consciousness. When Sunrise opened her eyes, she began to cry and moan, "Ohhh, God . . . he hit me."

"Can you walk?" Jacaranda asked. "We'll go to the bathroom."

"Oh, God, I want to go home," Sunrise said, once they were in the bathroom. Jacaranda had blood on her dress.

"He'll probably have the lock changed by now," Sunrise said.

She sat on the edge of the bathtub with her knees up to her chin and her elbows sticking out on either side so her shell-pink palms could cover her bleeding face, and she looked like a cricket-doll marionette with broken strings in a torn faded white dress with red blood on it.

It was all Jacaranda's *mis-en-scène* fault.

Jacaranda helped Sunrise sip the lukewarm white wine still in Jacaranda's glass, and said that it was all her fault.

Sunrise took a sip. Then she took a gulp. Then she said, "*Your* fault! It was *his* fault, the filthy bastard!"

Jacaranda's admiration for Sunrise grew.

"Would you like to stay at my place tonight?" Jacaranda asked. "I'll sleep on the floor; you can have the bed and Emilio, the cat."

"Oh, I can sleep anywhere," Sunrise declared, finishing off the wine. "I could sleep on this damn tile floor."

Sunrise rose from the bathtub, folded herself up in a corner on the cold tile with a towel for her blood and tears, and told Jacaranda to go away.

Back out in the party, the Temptations had taken control again and the empty circle was jammed with movie bodies in full swing. Everyone knew the way to dance was like black people did and they all danced that way.

"Is everything all right?" Shelby said, suddenly there, a worried frown on his face.

"What do you mean by 'all right?'" Jacaranda said. "I'm going home!"

"But, darling, you can't drive like you are now . . . And I can't leave this party, I promised Jack . . ."

"Naturally, *you* promised Jack so *I* can't leave. All alike!" Shelby tried to capture her, grab her arm. She pushed him away.

Outside, a Red & White Cab stood like a prop. The driver of the Red & White Cab, a junkie, realized Jacaranda's plight and drove her home without charge, explaining how his agent had taken his screenplay to London and any day the driver was expecting to hear that David Lean was interested. "It's in the bag," the Red & White Cab driver-writer-junkie said, "it's a dynamite concept."

"I love David Lean," Jacaranda said. *"Lawrence of Arabia,* I saw it fourteen times."

"I saw it eight," he said.

He walked her to her door and helped her open it, "Everything, uh . . . O.K.?" he asked.

"Everything is really fantastic," she replied.

It was 10 p.m.

At two o'clock that morning, she woke up and felt as if she were drowning in empty red blues, sorrows, and shames. But then she lost consciousness until 8 a.m., when she woke up and saw that her bed was still empty. (Shelby had a key, he could have crept into her tent; he'd done it before when they'd fought, and when they woke up together everything was fine.) She was so overcast with unparalleled blue-black guilt that the delicacies of sorrows and shames were thrown into shadow with the rest of the world. Everywhere she looked seemed to be The End.

Everywhere she looked seemed ended.

Shuffle Off to Mexi . . .

Jacaranda thought of Zack and Sunrise. She'd heard that they had fights like that all the time—the dope dealer was always humiliating Sunrise in public. Always kicking her out of Laurel Canyon. Two or three times a year, in fact.

Jacaranda decided to telephone Zack and ask him what the secret was—how could he and Sunrise be the way they were together and not kill themselves on purpose or by mistake? And how could it be that after all they'd been through, neither of them seemed to show scars—Zack was still as evilly youthful as always and Sunrise didn't look a day over thirteen and it seemed she never would. (Jacaranda, on the other hand, looked about forty.) And how could it be that they'd acted like such a normal well-resigned couple when they'd toasted on the third of July?

Jacaranda found not a crack of hope for herself and Shelby. She remembered that the way he'd looked at her the night before had the look of finality, that he wasn't going to subject himself to her wild mercurial tempers anymore. He was going to close off the lagoon, lose the map, swim alone.

Jacaranda telephoned Zack Birnbaum with the utter desperation of someone reaching for any kind of lifeline, even a telephone cord, 8 a.m. or not. In L.A., you don't telephone people at 8 a.m. after a party. She didn't care; she *had* to find out how Zack and Sunrise continued to carry on, after what Jacaranda had witnessed.

"Hello?" Zack said, sounding zippy and matter-of-fact.

"Oh," Jacaranda said. "Listen, Zack, I just called to find out how you and Sunrise can survive the way you treat her."

"Here, I'll let you talk to her," he said.

Sunrise was home? In the moment it took for Sunrise to come to the phone, Jacaranda felt rescued by a tear of hope in the otherwise seamless surface.

"*Oh*," Sunrise said, in a death-rattled groan. "God. Hi."

There were sharks.

"He's kicking you out?" Jacaranda said.

"He . . . he's given me fifteen minutes to pack and get out, and I only have seven dollars and forty cents and my . . . my friend isn't in town who I usually stay with and . . ." Sunrise swept out to sea, a sea of her own tears.

"Hey," Jacaranda said, acting as though it were "only a movie," a sound in her voice of carefree girlish abandon, tempting adventure, and other insanely inappropriate optimisms, what-the-hell taints, "why not let's go to Rosarita Beach, cha-cha-cha?"

"Where?" Sunrise's sobs stopped. "Rosarita Beach?" she asked, in a normal voice. "Where's that?"

"Mexico, kiddo, just a little south of ole Tijuana, just a lee'l north of Ensenada. I hear a couple of girls like us, fine-looking girls, have a good time, get abortion, information, see a donkey fuck a whore, the works."

"But . . ."—Sunrise blew her nose—"I've only got seven dollars and forty cents."

"Hey," Jacaranda said, "I've got an American Express card and the restaurant down the street will cash a check for me. I can get a hundred dollars, just like that." Jacaranda snapped her fingers, a motion that was lost on Sunrise.

"Baja?" Sunrise sighed. "I've never been to Baja. I've never even been to Mexico. In fact, I've never been further south than Huntington Beach. I'd love to go."

"Well, chickadee, I come get you in fifteen minutes, you be packed, we fly to the east, fly to the west, fly to the one we love the best—we fly *south*. To Rosarita!"

Jacaranda stuffed two tops and some jeans into a shopping bag and telephoned April to ask her to feed Emilio.

"How long will you be gone?" April asked. "Won't you miss Emilio?"

"If it's longer than a month or so," Jacaranda replied, "I'll send for him."

April did not *hate* Shelby the way she hated Max. April just didn't believe in the existence of Shelby. If Jacaranda was going away, it would be Emilio she would miss. Emiliano was probably Mister Right.

It was the Fourth of July. Jacaranda knew she could stay out of town at least till the fifth, and the fifth was a Monday, a Janet Wilton day.

La Jolla
(Shuffle Off to Mexico)

They dropped Sunrise's things off at her friend's garage—the one who was out of town—and hoped the boxes wouldn't be stolen. "But it's O.K. if they are," Sunrise said, "because I'm obviously not meant to have anything anyway."

Despite Sunrise's desperate words, her attitude was as jubilant as Jacaranda's. Sunrise was driving because Jacaranda was too terrified to drive on the freeway and Sunrise had driven lorries in London for roadies. Sunrise drove like a boy. "I learned to drive from my brothers in

Tucson," she said, slashing through the moribund Fourth of July traffic jam, making mincemeat of Porsches. Until the traffic stopped completely for one large Fourth of July hot set-a-spell couple of hours, Sunrise beat the odds like a gambler winning against the house.

The minute Jacaranda had seen Sunrise in person again, she'd realized that perhaps being in a country like Mexico, where they kidnapped people and where Orson Welles was the corrupt Chief of Police, was not a place to sail forth into. Jacaranda didn't want things to get more dangerous than they already had. There were enough sharks at home.

They were locked into the San Diego Freeway in a river of shiny metal hoods and sticky Fourth of July children. It was clear to Jacaranda that they more than likely might never survive to the next freeway exit, much less to distant Mexico.

"You know," Jacaranda said, "let's *not* go to Rosarita!"

"*Great!*" Sunrise agreed. "But can we just get farther south than Huntington Beach? I'd like to get farther south than that. That's all I ask."

"What about La Jolla?" Jacaranda suggested. La Jolla, the town she knew so well, Shelby Coryell's hometown, where she and he had seized moments of their adolescence to lie and hide and surf.

"Where's that?" Sunrise asked.

Jacaranda could see how Zack Birnbaum might think Sunrise was stupid, but Jacaranda could see how Sunrise was just innocent and uninformed. She drove like the wizard of machinery; she couldn't be *that* stupid.

"La Jolla's farther south than Huntington Beach," Jacaranda replied. "Just north of San Diego. We'll pass the unindictable co-conspirator's house."

"Oh, San Clemente," Sunrise said. "I wonder what he's doing today."

"Pondering," Jacaranda suggested.

"I bet he wears a suit on the beach," Sunrise mused.

Once Sunrise started talking, she spoke so normally one forgot she was just an ornament. Sometimes, Jacaranda got the feeling that Sunrise wasn't really a mute wild animal brought in on a leash at all.

"I just couldn't believe that you called," Sunrise was saying. "I heard you say 'Rosarita Beach,' and I know running away is just a childish escape, but to throw me out on a holiday weekend with no money . . . I *knew* last night this was going to happen but the minute the music started . . . Zack says I'm a *schwartza*, dancing just because there's music . . ." She eeled her way into the fast lane where the cars were moving at twenty miles an hour. "You know, Jacaranda, I'm gettin' too *old* to be out on the street."

"How old are you?" Jacaranda asked.

"Twenty-eight," Sunrise said.

"Oh," Jacaranda said. She didn't see a single sign of Sunrise's being twenty-eight. Sunrise only looked adult at all because she had breasts.

Jacaranda gazed at the head held in perfect posture, profiled toward Jacaranda throughout the trip.

Sunrise told Jacaranda the story of her name, about the man in Golden Gate Park, and the Be-In, and how her name was really Judy Corrigan. Jacaranda knew that Sunrise's name was *not* Judy.

"What's your name *really?*" Jacaranda asked.

"Chah," Sunrise admitted (pronounced like "jaw," only with a "ch" that sounded as though there were a "t" in front of it).

"Oh," Jacaranda said. ". . . Chah."

"But in school I was called Judy," Sunrise said, "and then I ran away when I was fourteen . . . I had it legally changed when I was eighteen."

"Well, you could always change it back," Jacaranda said. "Only forget that Judy stuff. Keep the Chah."

"Chah Corrigan," Sunrise Honey said. "It sounds like a Robert Mitchum movie."

"I love Robert Mitchum." Jacaranda sighed.

"Me, too." Sunrise sighed.

"Do you know 'Shuffle off to Buffalo'?" Jacaranda asked. Sunrise, it was revealed, could learn any song after hearing it once. In fact, she could just sort of imagine how a song *would* go. It was shocking each time she was right; it was shocking in the way that certain musicians just plunk out the melodies, chords, and all, and can't even read music, never "learned," just know.

Whoo, Whoo, *Whoo, Whoo,* Shuffle Off to Buffa...

I t was almost impossible to feel human compassion, plain humanity, toward Sunrise, Jacaranda suspected later on, especially if you were a human female. But that day Jacaranda could feel Sunrise's pulse. She could see it in the inside of her wrists, the lines where the blue blood flowed, the life. She could also hear and smell Sunrise up close in broad daylight, hear Sunrise's whooping wispy voice, which seemed so impossible when the rest of her was so miraculously ravishing.

Up close in broad daylight, Jacaranda could see how each of Sunrise's teeth was absorbed into the scallops of her healthy, childlike gums. (The first thing Jacaranda always got disillusioned about with ravishing beauties was their teeth; there are so many ways for teeth to go wrong. Jacaranda's teeth were all that was left of her first beauty.) Sunrise's teeth were broad and scalloped at the bottom; they were big teeth to go with her enormous smile. Sunrise's smile beat out daylight for first place. Oh, but Sunrise, Sunrise was flexible and light, not shatterable light. Sunrise had been smacked in the face the night before with a punch that would have broken one of those new polyurethane surfboards but had only puffed her face up and made it reddish (turning blue). Sunrise lived to see the sea the very next day; she hadn't ended up in the elephant graveyard. She was flesh and blood. She was a member of humanity worthy of compassion.

She and Sunrise were *lucky*. They had a hundred dollars and an American Express card and they were innocent virgins off on a gay adventure.

The Beautiful Friend

U p close in the sun-visor mirror, Jacaranda's face was a sordid record of reckless debauchery, especially in broad daylight on the Fourth of July. She began to wonder why Shelby hadn't left her to the sharks sooner. Her lips were chapped and her hair had been allowed to inch its way to its own natural color, which she saw in broad daylight was getting gray. She knew that her midriff was puckered with ripples of unsightly sights. And her eyes were always pinkish no matter how much eyeliner she put on. And she ought to have put more eyeliner on, but she was too lazy and didn't care. She just left herself as she was. She was, after all, a writer and they died earlier than anyone. It was truly simple.

It was amazing, therefore, that Jacaranda, whose beauty was impure and violently mortal, was still able to rise to most any occasion and, if there wasn't someone like Sunrise cluttering up the landscape, was usually able to be the most beautiful and fascinating woman in the room. Even after Jacaranda gained weight and her legs were scruffed with alcoholic black-and-blue stains, Etienne had always wound up with her. In the morning, Etienne would turn to Jacaranda's side of the bed with an expression of fearful trepidation that would dissolve as he said, "Oh, thank God, a beautiful friend."

Jacaranda, despite battering her body and mind against a brick wall the way she had for so long, could, from sheer sly remarks and sneaky asides, capture anyone's imagination. It was amazing that she could seem cheerfully indifferent to Max's waspishly alarming tactics, like "If I were you, Jacaranda, I wouldn't still try and get away with wearing *that*."

"Why not?"

"Well, I mean, there's not much room in this world for haggard mistresses . . ."

It was amazing that Shelby had loved her as long as he had. And it was amazing, considering the barge's low tolerance for intimations of mortality, that its passengers had let her stay on as long as they had.

Jacaranda didn't have to plan her suicide. She saw, looking in the sun-visor mirror up close in broad daylight, that she was committing it already.

The Colonial Inn

All the way to La Jolla, they tried to get off the freeway and take a normal street, but all normal streets ended in dead ends.

They figured out by the eleventh dead end that the *free*-ways were prisons, and if you tried to get out, there were only dead ends. To find this out on Independence Day was one of the reasons they fell back laughing. Their sides were hurting, so out of tone were their laugh muscles.

They'd finally agreed not to look at each other or they'd start laughing again, and as far as "progress" and "making good time" were concerned, they'd gone forty miles in four hours—you could walk it.

The freeway was like a taffy pull. They stopped at a motel for the night at Dana Point (south of Huntington Beach), a motel Jacaranda didn't recall because of the vodka. She woke up at 6 a.m., woke Sunrise up, and said, "If we hurry, maybe we can make it somewhere before the traffic clots."

"Clots?"

"Well, they're not going to let it bleed, are they?" Jacaranda asked reasonably. "When you try and get away, it's just dead ends."

"Don't you have a hangover?" Sunrise said, hustling into the car, a fast mover like Jacaranda.

"With vodka, I usually don't get hangovers, I just black out. If we hurry, maybe it'll go away."

"Oh," Sunrise said, lowering her eyes in silence.

There wasn't a single car on the freeway on July 5th, a Monday.

They arrived in La Jolla in time for breakfast and took a room at the right place for the occasion: the Colonial Inn. The Colonial Inn was a block from the ocean, and was empty, as far as they could tell, except for the man who told them the hotel was in escrow and was changing hands. He invited them (Sunrise had smiled) to go dancing that night with his friends. They said maybe.

All of La Jolla seemed to be empty, not just their hotel.

Their room was perfectly white, with bride's-veil nylon organdy curtains that billowed out in the sea breeze, the ocean being so nearby.

Sunrise went straight off to take a shower. Jacaranda left and returned from across the street, where she'd picked up two half-gallons of Iglenook Chablis, and poured herself a glass of cold wine. She looked out the window and tried to remember.

It came to her. At last.

It was Matisse, a Matisse she'd seen in a museum. It was a huge painting of a hallway looking into another room, which had a window that was open out onto the blue sky. It was the same wonderful gay protective singing sky. No danger could ever befall a person under a sky that color.

When Jacaranda had first looked at that painting, it had been a year since she'd abandoned the colors of art. Now it brought colors back to her and she teetered, for a moment, wondering whether she might not be better off being a Xeroxer and painting rather than Xeroxing and writing. But then, who else would get a sky that blue? Those skies had been done as well as they ever could be. All the art she'd ever done was but a thimbleful of color compared to one inch of this Matisse. Nobody was ever going to paint the way Matisse painted wallpaper on the walls of a room whose only occupant was a dog, asleep, under the table. Later, when she heard that Picasso was nasty about Matisse, she knew why. Here Picasso went to such trouble to touch all the bases, invent the twentieth century, paint ladies' faces in half, and Matisse sat inside a room that looked into another room where the window was open, with the sky that color blue. Picasso had been *through* the sky, come out the other end, dug to China with a child's shovel, and seen opposite skies . . . while Matisse just sat at home. And somehow *his* skies were bluer.

This particular feeling of loveliness, this virginal rapture from the sky, protective and simple, was all around, everywhere, permeating La Jolla with its pseudo-*Ramona* mission-Spanish name (for in actual Spanish there is no word "jolla"—there's a word "joya," which means jewel). None of this mattered. Historical accuracy fell by the wayside: the morning they arrived at the Colonial Inn, with their white room, everything was drawn anew, reborn.

SUNRISE HAD ONCE been a junkie, she had tracks on her leg, but she'd kicked, cold turkey, when she realized what she was doing.

Naked, out of the shower, those were her only scars. On her legs, they didn't show the way Jacaranda's life did on her face.

It was hard to believe, afterward, that it had taken only one day—the fifth of July—and two hundred dollars' worth of cocaine, to straighten out the most major flaws of both Jacaranda's and Sunrise's life.

Cocaine, Cocaine

Cocaine is sometimes a great drug for numbing human emotion long enough to discover the Actual Truth, to face it, and to feel fine for fifteen more minutes, until you either come down or can get some more cocaine.

In Southern California, the Actual Truth is not usually very distinguished and hardly ever does it offer the breadth and scope it does in Moscow or London or New York. In L.A. and just south along the coast, the Actual Truth is usually dull and shopworn, yet somehow, like the Actual Truth everywhere, nobody wants to know.

Sunrise's problem was kid stuff, if you asked Jacaranda, who said, "How can you stay there when that Zack hits you?"

"But I don't have any money," Sunrise said, chopping up two more pairs of cocaine lines on a hand mirror, with a razor blade, where the nylon organdy curtains blowing in the sea breeze couldn't brush it all onto the floor.

"Oh, anybody would hire you," Jacaranda said.

"I've tried modeling but my breasts are all wrong," Sunrise complained.

"What about a real job? You know, like a job job? Like where you make two hundred and fifty or so a week and go to work in the morning and behave?"

"Oh, I could never get one of those jobs." Sunrise sighed. "How could I ever pass those written exams?"

"How could you think Zack could be right about anything, much less about how smart you are! Not that you don't act dumb. God, that lip-gloss routine!"

"Oh, I know!" Sunrise cried.

Whenever Sunrise was all dressed up to enter a public place and impress people, she glazed on lip gloss, and her eyes went blank. This combined to make her look incredibly vacant and even more of an object than she already looked.

"I've just got to stop doing that," Sunrise said.

"And then, once you get a job, you can get your own apartment and own car and own cute little kitten," Jacaranda went on.

"But what'll I do before then?" Sunrise said, worried.

"What any other girl with no money does," Jacaranda said.

"Oh, but hooking, I don't know . . ."

"Call your mother."

"My mother?" Sunrise cried. "I haven't even seen her in fifteen years."

"Tell her you need five hundred dollars," Jacaranda said.

"*Call* her?" Sunrise said, stunned.

Sunrise got her mother's phone number from King City Information and, after two more lines of coke, she dialed.

Tears and money resulted.

And so, after promising to come visit her mother as soon as she could, Sunrise hung up, beaming.

"You can stay with me until everything is O.K.," Jacaranda said, adding, "See . . . your problems hardly last fifteen minutes once you don't take no for an answer."

Sunrise eventually spotted Jacaranda's problem from the mass of red-herring dead ends Jacaranda flooded into all of her conversations.

"Hey, wait a minute," Sunrise finally said. "Are you telling me that these publishing people have given you all this money and are waiting for you to go to New York? *That's* your problem?"

"It's so complicated," Jacaranda sighed, on her fifth glass of white wine. (Sunrise didn't really drink.)

"*How* is it complicated? You have the money, right? You're not afraid to fly, like that book, are you?"

"No, no, it's nothing like that . . ." Jacaranda grew mysteriously distant. "I'd rather not talk about it."

"Oh, right, it's something I'm too dumb to understand and that's why you won't tell me," Sunrise said, narrowing her peculiar eyes.

"Did you ever meet Max Winterbourne?"

"The man in the white suit who always hangs out with that Mr. Tension sex maniac?"

"Yeah!" Jacaranda exclaimed.

"Well?"

"Well, he's in New York!" Jacaranda explained.

"And?" Sunrise said, waiting for the rest.

"That's why I can't go," Jacaranda said.

"Oh . . ." Sunrise said at last. "Well, I hate to say this but I don't think I get it."

Jacaranda said, finally, "Maybe I should go to New York. Next week."

"What just happened?" Sunrise asked, wondering. "You changed."

"I think I'll go wash my hair," Jacaranda said.

"Oh, I've got some great shampoo," Sunrise said, moving smoothly into shampoo.

Jacaranda made plane reservations from the hotel in La Jolla—round trip to New York, one week away.

That night Jacaranda and Sunrise went for a walk along the beach and wound up at a party with a band where all the people were under thirty. The following morning, Jacaranda woke up with a long bruise on her thigh that looked like the one on her other thigh, only newer. She couldn't remember where either one had come from.

When they drove into L.A. the next day, the sky was wretched and damp. July was always the worst month. It had been a long time since Jacaranda had been out in the noonday sun without sunglasses. She couldn't remember where she had left them.

"You know, Jacaranda," Sunrise said, her attention mostly on passing a truck, "sometimes when you have had a little too much to drink . . ."

The truck started honking at them until the driver spotted Sunrise and veered way over to the right dangerously before he regained control. Sunrise went on talking:

". . . people who don't know how wonderful you are might get the wrong impression."

Jacaranda wrote that down; it was the most foolproof attack of persuasion she'd ever witnessed.

(It wasn't as spectacular as cocaine, but if forced to face the Actual Truth with only words between it and oneself, it would do quite nicely.)

Empty Windows

Shelby was never home when she called after the party. Every night, the week before she went to New York, she sat in her car across the street from his studio and looked into his dark windows.

His car was parked outside, but his apartment was always dark.

He was nowhere to be found.

TWO DAYS BEFORE she went to New York, Jacaranda stopped drinking.

PART II

New York, New York
(The Mysterious East Lures the Innocent Virgin)

On the plane, Jacaranda drank diet grapefruit soda.
She could later report to her friends that in New York City you couldn't be sure if what's driving you wide-eyed with savage impulses was the d.t.'s or simply the city itself.

Unlike the threadbare tradition of sanitariums or some quiet country retreat, where every symptom of withdrawing is framed by green pastures and happy trees, the first week of New York is the ninth circle of hell under any circumstance—so what was a little not drinking. Besides, everybody knows it's impossible not to drink in New York. It was just the place for most of the people Jacaranda knew, since anything impossible drew them to it in vast numbers. None of her friends could be bothered with something that was possible.

Jacaranda believed that in the world of airplanes there were only two kinds of luggage—carry-on or lost. She packed everything she thought she could possibly need for a week into one carry-on bag. And it wasn't that stuffed.

She wore loose cotton pants and loose smocky tops, which she knew weren't fooling anyone into thinking she was secretly thin underneath, but at least she wouldn't have to think about it all the time.

April had driven her to the airport and given her a paperback copy of *Winning Through Intimidation.*

"Here," April said, "you better read this before you arrive."

"I can't believe I'm going to New York like this—all by myself, sober—with Max there," Jacaranda said.

"How can you even consider anyone that *old?*" April had asked.

April looked more seaworthy than thou with her sailor pants, her dark brown hair with red streaks, and her skimpy body.

AS THE PLANE landed, Jacaranda vowed to bear in mind that New York was not L.A. That way she'd perhaps refrain from plunging headlong into tiresome remarks about dog-do on the sidewalks, or getting mugged in Central Park, or "the pace" being so frantic. She would not see immaculate freeways, girls in shorts on skateboards, or Thai food.

In the cab going into Manhattan, though, she allowed herself to inhale the skyscrapers across the East River, looking so empty and silent at 7 a.m. in the clear morning sun glaze. Already she felt the bristling of desire come flooding through her veins.

•

JACARANDA WAS LET off at a quarter to eight in front of the Essex, where she was to meet her friend Winifred Shaughnessy and Hudnut.

The way the morning struck the town was so beautiful it was much too hard to suffer from not drinking with any conviction. It was all she could do not to smile so much at people. She had not had a drink for three days. And now New York made her so glad she was sure it would be no trouble to take off into the air and fly.

She stepped into the Essex lobby, determined not to smile.

The Beach Boy Girls

Jacaranda had first met Winifred Shaughnessy in the offices of the rock-'n'-roll group for whom Jacaranda was trying to do an album-cover photo. Wini was seventeen then (Jacaranda was twenty); she was the receptionist. Even then, Wini was skeptical and unimpressed by Jim Morrison coming naked toward her in the street. She was skeptical and unimpressed by practically everything, and that made her indispensable in rock-'n'-roll. Wini was unimpressed by getting fired, so she would say anything, and because she never exaggerated and was correct in every detail, she was worth her unimpressed weight in gold.

She was darling, and men all loved her because she terrified them with her sharp tongue and big blue-gray eyes.

Other girls may have lolled around the outer office waiting for the objects of their groupie affections to pass by, but Wini, by the time she was eighteen and a half, knew the entire score. Nothing but worthy, decent intelligence and kindliness impressed Wini, and there she was, right in the middle of greasy ambition. She rose from being a hardworking receptionist to being an invisible secretary of state for a man who directed a vast rock-'n'-roll empire that covered three continents. He picked her out of his three offices of a hundred people because his talent was discovering talent. One day, Wini had just been another secretary; the next, she was . . . well, he told her she could have any title she liked. In the midst of rock-'n'-roll, especially, Wini shone out like the break of day.

Winifred had only this to say to Jacaranda: "You can stay with me if you want, I'm taking a suite near the Park, but one word—*one* smartass word—about Hudnut, and you're out."

Winifred had found her dog, Hudnut, in a trash can in some place like Hudnut, Idaho. He was only a puppy but his shining virtues were instantly apparent to Winifred, who had put him in her car and taken him home to Tarzana.

Hudnut stood down on the floor; each of his paws was ready to go. His tail had been stolen from a Ziegfeld Follies headdress or a romantic plumed-pen garret.

"Is that how he's turned out, I mean?" Jacaranda had asked when she first saw him.

eve babitz

"*Yes!*" Wini said. "And not another word!"

"But . . ." Jacaranda began.

"*No!* One more word and my dog and I are leaving," Winifred said, gathering her purse.

"Why should I say anything about Hudnut?" Jacaranda asked and assumed offended dignity. Jacaranda tried to like dogs but she just didn't like them; they barked. She liked cats; they purred. But she had agreed "not a word about Hudnut," and had said she would call up to Winifred's room when she got to the Essex that morning so they could have breakfast together. Wini had been in New York for two days before Jacaranda and had chosen the Essex with its $150-a-night rooms so that she would be right across the street from Central Park for Hudnut.

THE ESSEX IS a classical family-style sedate hotel. Wini was employed by rock-'n'-roll, but the corporation that owned her boss had more legitimate enterprises under its name, and the Essex thought Wini was somehow connected with one of the nicer businesses, like furniture manufacturing or oil transportation or graveyards. Otherwise Jacaranda and Winifred would certainly have been handed down to the Drake Hotel, a place more suitable for their obvious rock-'n'-roll inclinations, which, in the lobby of the Essex the morning Jacaranda arrived, glared like the only inaccuracy for miles.

They stood out. Winifred wore a Day-Glo baseball shirt with DODGERS scrawled in satin across the front, a

Dodger baseball cap, just plain jeans, and striped tennis shoes. Wini would have stood out as it was; she didn't need to be exaggerated by having Jacaranda next to her all draped in brooding mauve cotton that revealed a lot of cleavage. Winifred's carefree honey straight-valley hair (Winifred was a Beach Boy song) topped her off, and Jacaranda's recently grown-out hair had been newly cut and blondly streaked for New York and she looked much less raggedy than she had in La Jolla.

"Ahhh," the man at the desk said, "the young ladies from California. *Southern* California? Am I right?"

"Yes, this is Ms. Leven," Winifred said, "who'll be receiving calls in my suite."

Out of nowhere, three Bloody Marys tiptoed across Jacaranda's mind. It was only 8 a.m. (though five in L.A.). They tiptoed straight off the stage and into the opposite wing. She tried to bear in mind the skyline, how New York had looked that July morning, bombastically beautiful, glittery. She'd imagined New York could be that beautiful only when Sinatra sang "Autumn in New York" and about "glittering crowds and shimmering clouds in can*yons* of steel . . ."

Winifred had been to New York four times, but never ventured anywhere geographically outside the prescribed territory of rock-'n'-roll: fancy French restaurants and the music district. She'd never been south of Forty-eighth Street and never conceived of going even to make a historical pilgrimage to the home of Bob Dylan, the Village.

Jacaranda had been to New York before she had been on the barge. She'd visited relatives and made pilgrimages to Greenwich Village, which never seemed like the home of Bob Dylan to her. It was the home of Marlon Brando when New York was hot and Tennessee Williams made poetic sense and everyone listened to Charlie Parker, Mugsy.

The third time that Jacaranda had come, in her early twenties on groupie adventures, her ideas about California had been cemented. California was the only conceivable place on earth to be. Anyone who wasn't blind from New York had to flee to Hawaii and purge himself for a month in pure waters and gentle breezes.

THEIR GIGANTIC ESSEX room was on the twenty-seventh floor and looked out over nothing whatsoever except drone. The drone came up from deep within the stony island and tangled its Niagara Falls fury straight through to Jacaranda's newly stripped nerves, nerves unaccustomed to meeting the world without a drink. It was exquisite, the Marquis de Sade might have said—exquisite madness.

It had a debonair glaze to it, not drinking in New York, that flew in the face of every tenet of A.A. about how to stop drinking. She had not come to the toxic level where she'd have to be straitjacketed to keep away the pink spiders. There was still time, it seemed, to slip bareback onto the golden palomino and ride into the sea, through a tangle of mazes, through New York. She had no exact idea how addicted she was or how advanced her case of alcoholism had become. But that morning on the twenty-seventh floor at 8:15, she knew she was doomed if she didn't change her idea of glamour.

Heretofore she'd lived with an image of champagne sipped from the glass slipper and an idea, too, about the seacoast of summer with cool white wine and hot white love. She'd even liked the one where decadence has so set in that only gin works in the end. She had lived for a long time with similar notions about cigarettes—Bette Davis striking matches, inhaling. But smoking . . . Etienne didn't smoke. Hardly anybody on the barge smoked, and they could afford every unfair advantage on earth. If Etienne no longer existed on his two packs of Egyptian cigarettes a day, then *no*body could smoke. At twenty-four, Jacaranda saw that cigarettes were *not* debonair props of leisure; they were what poor people grasped—like eating lead paint—to do *some*thing. Etienne quit without missing a beat. He continued to light ladies' cigarettes with the same instinctive seriousness. It was just that he himself didn't . . . "you know . . . smoke and so forth." Jacaranda had asked Etienne, "How did you stop?"

"It was quite simple," he told her. "I simply stopped."

That was when Jacaranda "simply stopped," too. It seemed to her that she'd been smoking *in order* to get through the days, not that her days were ornamented by cigarettes. Later she heard that kicking methadone was worse, that for days it made your bones feel like melting molten lead, and she was willing to admit the possibility that there might be something worse than quitting smoking, but she doubted she'd ever enjoy the opportunity of comparing the two. As far as she was concerned, nothing would ever be worse. Especially not a namby-pamby thing like not drinking for a week in New York City.

And she was right.

Compared to not smoking, not drinking—even when thrust naked into the New York drone—was a lead-pipe cinch.

It was made more difficult because Jacaranda knew that right nearby somewhere on the barge Etienne and Max were getting their kicks from champagne on up. Probably lots of that pure unstepped-on merc (cocaine undiluted by baby-laxative). And Mandrax (English methqualone, which was even more vile than its fraternal American twin, Quaaludes). And of course, there'd be those brandies and those cocktails before dinner and red wine that tastes like the sun setting in heaven.

Jacaranda felt another urge, not the soft tiptoe of the three Bloody Marys, but an urge to "just call Max and see if he's in"—an ambivalent urge—the most irresistible kind. Just because it was 8:15 in the morning. He would call *her*. He had called her at less civil times when he'd wanted to talk to her.

But at 8:15 in the morning, cold sober and with no prospect of four or five Bloody Marys, Jacaranda was unable to think of anything more frivolous or enchanting to speak of than a bald plea for mercy, and though Max, in a lot of ways, was not "masculine," if you asked him for mercy, it was a cue for him to do you in.

As Jacaranda looked out the sealed New York window at a blank wall, with a bagpipe drone that had begun to scrape against her naked ears, the idea occurred to her that she might go all the way through New York and not see Max at all. Of course, it was impossible, but then, what wasn't.

"The man's a monster," Winifred said when Jacaranda explained how Max would set her up. "He's a genius at it."

"Maybe I'm in love with the genius part," Jacaranda groaned.

"Maybe you're in love with melodrama," Wini suggested.

But most people had a double thought about the Jacaranda and Max Thing. They thought that Jacaranda and Max had been lovers for five years. And they thought Max was gay. They were wrong about the first, of course. Jacaranda had never even kissed Max, for fear of being scarred for life by his acid tongue. As for the second, that Max was gay—little by little over the years, Jacaranda began to decide that whatever Max was, he certainly was not at all happy or glad, and he seemed, the more she knew him, not to want anything to do with sex at all. He seemed to want to be included in the family of man without the inexplicable sex part. The family of man he was with, lead by Etienne, wasn't indulgent of subtle shadings: either a man liked to fuck women or he liked to fuck men. Jacaranda began to suspect that Max's secret, his Big Mystery, was his liking of lively dinner conversation. He had an uncanny ability to pick out who would go with whom and to introduce them. The men and women Max introduced to each other practically tripped over their own shoes falling in love on their way to bed. People called Max a pimp for his delicate games, at which point Jacaranda began to think those on the barge were every bit as dim-witted as the ordinary mortals on dry land they so adroitly avoided.

Jacaranda had come to believe that there were some men—Max, perhaps—who understood sex perfectly and wouldn't get near it.

Winifred had known about Max and Jacaranda—what "people" thought and what Jacaranda told her (the melodramatic truth). The one time Wini had actually met Etienne, he'd just come in from tennis and a shower. He wore what he insisted was a bathrobe but what was a dressing gown, and Wini fell back in amazement at the gorgeousness of Etienne's narrow shoulders and lizard amber hands.

AS THEY BREEZED into Central Park, Jacaranda and Wini watched Hudnut dash into big trouble, two German shepherds and some kind of Airedale, and it was touch and go for a moment or two.

"He likes it here," Wini said, walking along.

"So do I," Jacaranda said. "You won't mind if I have d.t.'s, will you? Don't you think it's great that I won't be drinking?" Jacaranda asked.

"Great?" Wini asked.

"Well, I mean, I won't be so drunk all the time."

"You're fun when you're drunk. The life of the party," Wini said. "But I gotta go to bed early anyway . . ."

"You don't even care if I get d.t.'s," Jacaranda complained. "I mean, here I am going to pieces over the noise already and you think I'm one of those Watteau ladies on a swing."

"No, I don't," Wini said. "I just think you've got great frames."

"Frames?"

"Didn't you once tell me that theory of yours about frames, and how the bigger the frame that you put around something, the more compelled people are to notice what's in it?"

"Yeah," Jacaranda said. "People just *have* to look it it."

"Packaging, I guess," Wini said.

Hudnut pranced into view.

Suddenly Jacaranda had grave doubts.

"Oh," Jacaranda sighed, "if only I had a bottle of brandy."

"A bottle of brandy! You want me to go get you one?" Winifred asked.

"You know," Jacaranda said, looking up at the sky, "I

could be mistaken, but does it look to you like it's going to be a nice day?"

"A very nice day," Winifred said.

The Mysterious East
Versus a Constitutional

I t was nine o'clock and Wini went in to take a shower and shampoo her hair. (She shampooed her hair every day. Jacaranda thought that if there was one sign of opulence in Southern California, it was clean cotton clothes and shampooed hair—people used up so much water and gas and electricity keeping their little T-shirts and denim pants, their hair, spanking clean.)

Jacaranda began mooning around the room as the din grew more and more, now that the traffic had become serious. Dandy little martinis danced across the stage.

Jacaranda was in New York, and if that wasn't bad enough, she couldn't get an exact picture—now that she was there—of why she'd come. Janet's voice, was that it? But when Jacaranda had telephoned her agent to say she was finally actually coming, Janet had simply said, "Fine, where will you be staying?"

She looked around the good-mannered Essex room. Hudnut, flopping his dangerous plumed tail, seemed perilously close to sweeping everything off the coffee table in front of the polite settee.

New York was taking the opportunity to add a demented side to what she was doing by being—itself—crystal clear, physically. Already, that morning, Jacaranda had seen outlines on leaves a block away, shimmering. The weather was elating, glittering. It went against bemoaning the here and now in the worst way. One practically had to be crazy to resist the light as it dappled the horses and carriages south of Central Park across the street. Even the taxicabs looked like musical notes. All her fourteen-year-old cravings for "compares with Mott Street in July . . ." And this *was* July! The very July from the song! Every skyscraper penthouse overlooking a Broadway movie where George Sanders tells her, "Someday, my deah, this shall all be yours . . ." It was uphill work being a wet blanket with Cole Porter in charge of the scenery. But Jacaranda bemoaned away.

"You can take a bath or shower if you want now, while I'm talkin' on the phone," Winifred said, since no girl from the valley could possibly imagine going through the day wearing what Jacaranda was wearing, what she'd already worn on the plane. Jacaranda took a bath.

She had to admit that at least when you didn't drink, your eyes didn't become pink. When you didn't smoke, of course, so many improvements bustled into view you felt like an unauthorized testimonial to Clean Living. But when you didn't drink, it only took two days for the very color she was applying to her cheeks to leave her eyes. Not that she shouldn't be compensated for her loss of personality, which she realized was closing in on her. (Rambunctious double-bourbon good-fellowship just collapses without the double bourbon.)

"You ready?" Winifred called. Wini was newly clad in a pair of overalls and a Day-Glo orange T-shirt.

"Ready?" Jacaranda said. "How could I *ever* be ready for this?" She was too overweight to go around in overalls. She wore one of the floppy cotton outfits, layered and unwrinkleable, that she had brought on the plane.

When she broke apart from Wini and Hudnut at 9 a.m. on the corner of Sixtieth and Fifth Avenue, her Beach Boy clout did, too. Jacaranda was supposed to meet Wallace Moss at Dobson & Dalloway at ten, and she decided to walk. She did not expect her hands to start shaking while she was walking down the street but she couldn't help it. A sort of slanted sunbeam just wasn't warm enough in New York when you're not drinking and it's July. If she went into a nice bar and got a nice Irish whisky, her hands would stop shaking but that would give all the girl scouts in A.A. a smug moment, so she went into a "health-food store" (a New York City–style health-food store) where, rather than sell chocolate, they sold marzipan. The ray of sunlight that focused on the HEALTH FOOD sign was one of those artful nudges from Above—the bar next door was lost in gloom.

Jacaranda, having been through everything about dreary health fads in California, had finally gotten over her native repugnance by reading Adelle Davis's *Let's*

Get Well. It was easy to see why Adelle had the whole health field all to herself. The trouble with any salvation usually is that it's not at all funny; her book was a lot more chipper than most salvation prose. The others, with their "healthful benefits," don't know it, of course, but the word "beneficial"—even when applied to a baked potato with chocolate fudge for dessert—causes people's spirits to droop. Somehow, Adelle Davis managed to curb her "beneficials." She made good health sound like something to enjoy.

Once, long before Jacaranda had come to New York, she'd looked up "alcoholism" and found that Adelle recommended dolomite, because it had magnesium in it. Adelle said that schizophrenics and women about to have their periods have the same lack of magnesium and ought to take dolomite, too. But Jacaranda wondered if it was any good for trembling hands.

"Got any dolomite?" she asked the dusty old marzipan man.

"Dolomite?" He hesitated. "Oh . . . yes, I believe I do have some. In the back."

He puttered into the storeroom and came out with a bottle of dolomite. Jacaranda paid two dollars for a hundred, and took nine in the bar next door. The water cost a dollar. She didn't dare order just water, so she ordered a whisky with a water chaser (could she order a beer with a water chaser?) and left without drinking the whisky, left the whisky orphaned on the bar, and went back out into the "We'll have Manhattan . . ." morning.

Jacaranda now had forty-five minutes to make it to the the East Side of town where Dobson & Dalloway's offices were. Forty-five minutes for pondering upon why Wallace Moss would want to see her. Why didn't he just read the book and leave her out of it? She pondered as she walked, her body slanted forward as though against a blizzard, her eyebrows all frowned up.

She looked as if she had just been fired, rather than like a lucky youngish author who was about to advance her career. Hemingway, in his typical grandiose way, said that courage was grace under pressure. It occurred to her that, contrary to Hemingway, unless you're going to be a bullfighter, you don't need grace under pressure. You need grace in between pressures—getting from pressure to pressure—not when your house falls down on you. The dolomite had already started to work. Jacaranda's hands had stopped shaking and her mind started running. She could tell she was better, because a healthful glow of beneficial hatred reared its head.

She passed the booty of objects, the shops with everything there is in them, the silk and pearls and cloisonné and bias-cut satins. She began feeling an even finer-tuned rage against material East Coast diamondy objects.

Every time Jacaranda came to an intersection, the fanatical traffic and single-minded pedestrians forced their way into her mind. She wasn't about to even think, How can people live this way? She wasn't to think in clichés. Most of the people in New York probably lived on twenty mattresses of Sinatra's "glittering crowds and shimmering clouds . . ." Jacaranda thought of ninety reasons for "It's so exciting, I couldn't live anyplace else, even though I know the place is . . ."

Jacaranda's face mirrored, over and over in shop windows, how vulnerable and foreign she was. Her face looked almost as if five years had been torn away from it, like a bandage, and left raw. It was not a bad look once you put lipstick on, which she did the minute she found a ladies' room.

It was as though in return for putting together and sticking into an envelope and mailing to Janet Wilton what turned out to be Her Book, she'd been given nine Golden Clouds just for acting like a regular person. And now that she'd dragged herself into Businessland, they had painted the whole place and got a new sky. All she had to do was move an inch and they assumed she had won the mile.

Jacaranda anthropomorphized, awarded with human motivations, just about everything. To her, even her luck or fate or destiny was out of an Olympus with ulterior motives. Of course, there may have been a larger plot behind it all. But so far, it looked as if those in charge dashed in at the last minute and were too busy to see what she really deserved. When the gods on Olympus discovered the mistake, she hoped they would understand that she hadn't sent it back because she didn't know their address. Luck certainly had gone unfairly to others, she decided.

It was probably meant for Shelby, she thought, not thinking about him as Max's ghost, as she now and then did. Shelby was different from Max. He seemed born to accept good fortune and not grouse about how it wasn't his. If Shelby had been given an Oscar, he would have danced all night and gone out first thing the next day to buy a stand for it. Jacaranda, on the other hand, would spend the next three nights awake trying to think of what to say when the TV cameras arrived to catch her face as she was told there'd been an unfortunate error. Shelby had grace from pressure to pressure. If only Jacaranda wasn't so addicted to his flesh, she was sure she would find someone more befitting, someone who appreciated her, someone who knew what Dobson & Dalloway meant.

It was all very well for Jacaranda to smirk about the weather and the newness of New York, about how much better a city it was, but no one—no one except for Wini and her parents and some of her friends from New York—knew what Dobson & Dalloway was. To Shelby Coryell, it was just a name he'd heard, just another publishing company. But to her Dobson & Dalloway was the last of the gentlemen publishers. The firm was so substantial in its reputation, its history, of fostering little-known writers that Dobson & Dalloway publishing Jacaranda was like Bach asking her to study composition with him. For Jacaranda to be accepted by them meant that she could get hit by a bus and not die.

It seemed as though nothing Jacaranda could do in the world of writing would induce publishers to say no, once Janet Wilton was her agent. She still couldn't imagine Janet very well; she was that voice on Monday morning. (Janet must have a list to begin each week's work—telephoning writers to kick them out of bed.) Everything Jacaranda had done before she had Janet Wilton for an agent had been provincial, but from the moment Janet Wilton had said "I'm going to represent you," life had changed. It shifted into first, and began going up a steep hill. Now Jacaranda was resting on a temporary plateau (Janet acted as though it were temporary) high above the hurly-burly of Jacaranda's normal (before she met Janet) life. Jacaranda was going up so fast she felt she might die of the bends.

LONG BEFORE SHE met Wallace Moss, she was his fan. Ever since, in fact, she realized what he was doing with her manuscript. Janet Wilton had said, "He's the best editor in the city. I could have sold it to three other places, but I know those guys over there and I think you could have conned them. Wally I know you can't con."

"Why?"

"Because he's too smart for you," Janet explained.

By the time Jacaranda arrived at the bottom of the enormous building that housed Dobson & Dalloway, it was 9:45

and she was, as usual, early. Jacaranda had come to realize that only insane people get to places early but still she did it.

She looked up and suddenly the sidewalk seemed to slither out from under her as though it were an earthquake, but then it slid back.

Oh, God, she thought.

Well, she'd never know if it was the not drinking or the prospect of meeting someone she couldn't con. At least it wasn't an earthquake.

The Skeleton Team Olympiad

Jacaranda stared up at the building, which was fifty stories high.

When she got to the forty-fourth floor, Dobson & Dalloway hadn't even been lit up yet. She was there before the janitor. Only the daylight, shafting in from the windows (the walls were all glass on the outside), lit the reception area with no receptionist.

The place was bleak because the windows were tinted gray, so the daffy sunshine made no impression against the cream carpets and tastefully cream walls and "woodwork" (there was no wood; the building was too new). Not a creature was stirring or even stirred until 10:05, when the receptionist arrived and apologized for Wallace, who, she said, "is always early, I don't understand why he's not here now."

Jacaranda asked where the ladies' room was so she could go hide. She stayed in there while the lights on the floor came on. There were signs over the washstands saying: "Anyone having contact with Terry M. in the last month, please have gamma globulin shots: she has hepatitis." Another said: "Women who flush Kotex down toilets are a danger to the community."

Jacaranda looked at herself in the mirror and thought that putting Sunrise-like lip gloss on her made her actually look much better than usual, and she decided to add mascara and eyeliner. Then she put on more lip gloss. Too studied. She removed the lip gloss. It seemed as if she'd been there forever by the time she coolly ventured back out into the cream hallway, where it was now 10:15. She could hear a phone in the distance.

At the middle of the hallway, coming out of a cubicle, was a medium-sized, light-haired young man. He looked so out of place behind his serious glasses that it was almost as though he'd stepped out of a Giotto into a Wall Street law firm. When he spoke, however, these peculiar fancies were swept clean and it was clear that here it was 10:15 a.m., New York City, and there was nothing of Assisi about him.

"Are you— ?" he asked.

Wallace Moss seemed aslant; his voice—which Jacaranda had heard over the phone enough—sounded uneasy. Maybe he didn't know how to pronounce her name, she thought.

"Jacaranda Leven," she said, standing outside the ladies' room, craven with second thoughts about that whisky she'd left just sitting there in that bar. Or the removed lip gloss. She added, "Yes, I'm—"

Jacaranda sailed down the hall and shook Wallace's hand. It was her first smoothly risen-to occasion. She wanted to run back home to L.A. right away. Her heart was left down on the first floor—in the lobby—along with what little soul she had. What sailed down the hall on the forty-fourth floor were her body and brains, a skeleton team.

"I'm sorry I'm late," Wallace apologized, nodding at the clock, which said he was fifteen minutes late. "And I haven't even had my second cup of coffee yet. It'll be ready in a minute." His voice sounded overly polite.

"I was early," Jacaranda said. "I'm *always* early."

Jacaranda wondered if he was going to loosen up or if she would have to be nervous around someone equally nervous the whole time. The least he could do was be obviously robust.

He was leading her into his office. He really didn't look as if he belonged on Wall Street, because they wore ties down there, she'd heard, and suits—they dressed like Etienne, only murkier. Wallace wore jeans and a T-shirt, and a plaid short-sleeved shirt over it unbuttoned. It was his glasses—his firm, no-nonsense, stable, tinted glasses— that had made her think of money and business, Wall Street no-nonsense associations to her.

A slab of tinted window faced New York City, the East River, blocks of Industrial Revolutionary architecture.

"It's ready," the receptionist called, and Wallace went to get them both coffee. That's what she needed, she thought, more coffee.

How provincial she'd been, back in Los Angeles, thinking about Dobson & Dalloway, imagining that they were straight out of nineteenth-century London like her heroines. She'd imagined that writing books was to get out of the present and into a time when poise was the acme of life's ambitions. She'd expected something to go with her croquet-tea party. A watercress sandwich. But then, a watercress sandwich would never buy a book like hers, which dealt with the latest debaucheries in no uncertain terms: the life that Colman and the movie-movie people were leading, that quiet life with all that money and all those flowers and those blue pools and naked bodies. Those Oscars in the bathrooms. Those women, her age and a little older, who'd all gone crazy or who were hooking in the Polo Lounge or who were married to real old movie stars and had to look old too, to match. Those occasional men of genius who, like one friend of hers, could cast the right person for the right part and never miss—*never*. Jacaranda had written one story about his telephone book, the tiny names, the hundreds and hundreds of tiny names, and how he didn't drink or smoke or stay up late—he was always reading scripts, going to basketball games, or was in the company of three girls competing for the same part—in his bed.

Handing her her coffee, Wallace said, "If I had had my second cup, I would have told you how exciting it is to have you here at last and how honored I am to meet you."

"Oh," Jacaranda said. "Honored?"

"Please don't be cute"—he shrank—"until after I've had this." He sat down in his chair and concentrated on his coffee.

She would have hated him for saying something charming and something mean like that while she was bleeding illusions all over the wall-to-wall cream carpet. But maybe he didn't see her illusions, being invisible the way they were; maybe he thought she was who she wrote about. And she *was*. Only not just yet. She really didn't have enough of herself to hate him properly; all she knew was that she *would* have hated him if she were truly there.

She felt her strength drain even more, so that she hardly had it in her to wish she'd never come. And then she remembered Janet Wilton's by-the-way remark about "Don't try and con Wally, he's too smart." Janet had added, "Save it for the magazine editors," but Jacaranda didn't have to con magazine editors—magazine editors *liked* her. She didn't know *what* Wallace Moss was thinking. And although the most overall serious fearful person so far in Jacaranda's life was Janet Wilton, it now struck Jacaranda that Wallace—"Wally"—was what stood between her and her words being printed in a book. A book. Her very own book. What if he didn't like her? She *was* too fat. What if she found out he'd made a dreadful mistake; what if he firmly but politely, at the end of their meeting, told her that after all, she understood of course, she *did* understand, that Dobson & Dalloway was an established publishing house, a place with dignity and history, and they just couldn't publish her—and he'd look through his glasses kindly and say, "You *do* understand, don't you?"

Only it wouldn't be a question. It would be a flat declaration. They'd pay her off and wash their hands of her. They'd cut their losses.

She really wished she'd never come.

Her hands weren't shaking. That was something. In fact, there was nothing, as she sat there silently, except her white knuckles around the paper coffee cup, to give away who she was. How could she *not* try and "con Wally?" If he knew who she was, he'd take it all back. Things seemed thrown into reverse for a moment, and then she realized they were merely in very slow motion. It was the first time in her life that "the minutes passed like hours" sounded like a description, not a timeworn exaggeration. The seconds passed as if they were going backward, time came to such a standstill.

The memory of however long it was burned in Jacaranda's visual text. It had the strident fictitious clarity of things she remembered eating when she was fourteen, cherry snow-cones on the beach. It stuck to her mind like tar.

eve babitz

It was the window, mostly. Outside the window, beyond the floor-to-ceiling tinted glass, thickening to the docks in grimy greasy nineteenth-century chains and machinery, were a few blocks of Manhattan. But the day, the day sun just zigzagged light off all the surfaces like diamonds. The East River, the one she'd heard was almost as poisonous as the one on the other side that wasn't east, looked like the Green Danube, looked like a shiny green floor ready for the waltz to begin, anticipating a young girl with damp ringlets, an innocent virgin, in the arms of a serious young man with natural good manners to one-two-three, one-two-three their way across its madly obliging surface.

The window itself was perfectly set in. There were no little chipped corners the way there were in L.A., where on even the newest buildings you had to accept little cracks and things from the earthquakes. The wall-to-wall carpet came perfectly to the edge of the window wall and perfectly, hard-edge, stopped.

Inside the window, the place was a mess. Stacked up were bundles of papers, dirty-looking papers, smaller than the bundles Jacaranda remembered from grammar-school paper drives, but tied with twine the same way those papers had been. They looked more the size of manuscripts.

They *were* manuscripts.

Oh, no!

Time proceeded to inch forward once again. It had to. She looked up from her coffee and smiled her nice white-teeth invincible smile at Wallace Moss, who was, after all, only a man.

"You mean, you read all these things?" she asked, waving her hand with a sort of languid Garbo carelessness that made people think she was graceful. "How can you stand it?"

"It's . . ."—Wallace Moss finished his coffee and looked over the top of his glasses, his chin tucked into himself, his posture rotten—"interesting."

"Well," Jacaranda said, "I guess by the time they get to you, they're pretty well sifted. I mean, agents don't send you crap, right? And they have readers here."

"Agents *do* send me crap," he said. "But still . . . it's interesting."

He looked up at her out of his lowered lashes, his poor posture enabling him to turn his slightly balding light-haired head into an object of sexual thoughts, and then, when he smiled, of course, he looked so young . . . No wonder she was getting this under-the-eyelashes treatment, she decided; the bastard was probably a Scorpio, trying to take her prisoner. She gave him the rest of her coffee.

Jacaranda wondered how she was going to get this impossible person to like her so she could breathe normally instead of taking the shallow little pitter-patter breaths she'd been taking. Sitting around unable to breathe, with just your brain and body, was bad for her nerves. Her nerves were already about to retire, what with not drinking, no clichés, and . . . she couldn't remember the other one. Oh, calling Max. She was not calling Max. Well, she could actually feel the sound good sense in not calling Max as far as her nerves were concerned. It was one of the first times she actually experienced what she knew, intellectually, to be true, which was that the telephone is an instrument of the devil.

She hated and didn't want to seduce, but Wallace Moss *had* to like her—it wasn't "important"—he *had* to. Otherwise nothing could go anywhere. They *had* to be able to laugh at something together or take flight over something or . . . *something!* She didn't know exactly what was going on, but she didn't have Shelby and she didn't have the barge; she had the book and he *had* to like her. (At least she had been able to give him her coffee.) Wallace squinched up her coffee cup and threw it into his wastepaper basket. He pulled himself to his feet, slouching.

"Why don't I take you around," he said, "and introduce you to some of the people you'll be working with here? They've been anxious to meet you for a long time."

"Yeah, well, I . . ." Jacaranda couldn't go into the con she'd used on Janet Wilton. It wouldn't work. Wallace Moss wasn't going to stop and listen to her lame excuses; she'd have to figure out vigorous healthy excuses. "I, uh"—she paused—"was terrified."

"Terrified?" He stopped; they were going out his doorway.

"You know, petrified with fear?" she elaborated.

"*Terrified?*" He seemed stumped.

"Yeah. Like that if I came and people met me they'd change their minds?" She filled in the details. "Like you?"

"*You* were terrified of *me?*" he said. "But I loved your book!"

"Well, yes, I know, but I mean, that was just my book . . ." Jacaranda couldn't look at him, her eyes were locked onto her feet.

"*Just* your book?" He was quieting down but his voice was still riddled with shock and amazement and he was still standing tensely in the doorway.

"And you know," she added, so he'd understand, "I don't want to talk in clichés, but people from New York sometimes are sort of . . . *mean.*"

"Mean?"

"Well, I used to have a lot of friends from New York and—it just got to be too hard. That's how I got so fat," she ended. "They were very pushy."

"You're telling me you don't want to talk in *clichés* and you're telling me New Yorkers are pushy?" He looked at her, straight at her, full face, making her look at him and pulling her eyes up from her cold feet.

He liked her! She knew it all at once.

She looked straight through his tinted glasses, tinted like the window, into his plain gray eyes.

He smiled. He was so young. She had noticed that from the start, of course, but so close this way in the doorway, she knew it all at once.

Wallace led her out of his office and into the hallway, turning his back on her for the first time, a gesture of trust. It crossed her mind that maybe her not coming to New York all those months had not hurt Wallace's feelings exactly but had made him suspicious. Maybe, it crossed her mind, *he*—and Dobson & Dalloway in general—expected writers to breeze through New York and up to the forty-fourth floor, shake a few hands, show their manners . . . Of course, these thoughts were only idle notions, passing fancies, and Jacaranda viewed them as such.

But afterward—when she was to remember that morning and the sound of Wally's voice as he repeated *"Terrified?"* and *"Just* your book?"—it crossed her mind again that there might be something to that idea, idle fancy or not.

The Mysterious East Meets an L.A. Orange

She resumed wishing she'd never come.

Even with Wallace's back toward her, she thought it was just too hard being without her heart and soul, and having her breath so shallow. She felt as though she'd been in front of a firing squad that had changed its mind. And she just wished she hadn't come, even if Wallace Moss *did* like her. She could have gotten him to like her writing letters, she felt, and now she was going to have to meet all these other people. She wished she'd stayed home with Emilio.

She wished the windows weren't tinted gray, too.

Wallace turned right in to an office just twelve feet or so down from his. It was just like his, with that window for the far wall, only it looked bigger because it wasn't a mess. It was warm, cheery, and welcoming.

"This is Lloyd Cavendish," Wallace said, "our head of publicity."

"You've *come!*" Lloyd Cavendish cried. "You've actually come to New York. You know, after reading your book, I could hardly stand this place myself and I kept telling people the reason you didn't come was because you were in paradise and to read your book . . . And when they said they'd read your book and loved it so much they wanted to meet you, I told them you'd *never* leave L.A. And why *should* you? My dear, you really can *write!* You *really* can! *I* loved your book first, of course—I was the first to read it—but now with everyone in love with you, I feel I'll be lost in the shuffle . . ." (He was just like Max; her heart was flying to him. Indeed, by the time he was finished with his beautiful tapestry, Jacaranda's heart was up on the same level as the rest of her.)

Lloyd Cavendish looked like a cowboy from the fjords of Norway. He had pale blond hair, a silvery mustache, and dancing merry light blue eyes. Jacaranda was entranced, enchanted, spellbound. It was all she could do to keep her mouth from dropping open and staying that way, as if in a hypnotic trance. It was an effort to blink. It always happened to her; she didn't even need a kiss.

eve babitz

". . . and," he was continuing, "now you *are* come at last. You're *here!*"

(With that, her soul joined them.)

Wallace led her back into the hall. A woman who was about Jacaranda's age approached them. She was what Jacaranda thought of as "one of those Vassar graduates who can spell from birth."

"I'm so glad to finally meet you," Claudia Reilly said, shaking her hand and looking actually rather kinder than someone born to spell.

"Oh, thank you," Jacaranda said. (A rock-'n'-roll star had once told her that when a person likes what you do, all you can say, basically, is "Thank you.")

"And I know it's going to do well."

"Oh, well, really thank you," Jacaranda said.

"The funniest part was that casting-director person," Claudia said. "He was my favorite."

"I didn't realize people would be having favorites," Jacaranda said to Wallace as she followed along, her heart and soul and brain now up past the fiftieth floor and out the top, roving around in the wind of New York's glamorous beauty, the day of gloriousness and delight after all.

"WHY DON'T YOU make your phone calls while I finish up a few things," Wallace said, steering Jacaranda into an empty office, with a phone, a desk, and a chair, next to his. "And then we'll go meet Janet Wilton for lunch."

"You know, I've never met her," Jacaranda said. "Well, once, but all I remember are ruby earrings."

"But you *know* her, don't you?" he said. He'd met a lot of writers and he'd managed to stay pretty distant, but Jacaranda had come sliding in there in lavender clothes, with coffee she didn't drink and stories (*"Terrified?"*), and the next thing he knew she'd pulled at his heartstrings and she knew he had heartstrings, so he must have a heart. Most of the writers he worked with didn't know that. And now, having seen his heartstrings, she flagrantly avowed that she didn't even know her own agent, Janet Wilton, whom *everyone* knew.

Wallace Moss had never been to Elaine's, rarely went to literary parties, and never cross-indexed his life and friends—people he spent the weekends with didn't know what he did all day at work. Janet Wilton, of all the agents, was the only one who could get Wallace Moss down from the forty-fourth floor at lunchtime. So how on earth could it happen that Jacaranda, who was an author of Janet Wilton's, didn't know her?

"I don't know her," Jacaranda explained. She just couldn't contain herself she was so high on joy and gladness; it felt like Christmas, age eight, and she knew she was driving Wallace crazy. "I met her once. She gave me her card. That was more than a year ago. She calls me on the phone. She's very abrupt. She calls at seven in the morning. She's going to a psychiatrist, I found that out—what they call 'professional help?' And I don't have any professional help so I'm at her mercy, which is why I wrote the book. If I ever get enough money, I'm getting professional help, too. Fight fire with fire is what they tell you."

WALLACE MOSS LEFT Jacaranda—the Innocent Virgin versus the Phone—in an empty office looking out over the Green Danube; Jacaranda looked at the instrument of the devil, all alone. A moment of decision. She could call Max and wreck everything, go over and have nineteen Bloody Marys, a gram of coke, and catch the clap from some darling English prince, or she could gloat. Max would love being in on her success; he loved being in on things before they happened. The only time he liked being anywhere was before it happened. Jacaranda figured she had about four months before it happened with the book. She'd have four months of Max's undivided attention and then, depending on how it happened, he might stick around so he could be there before it happened again. If things didn't go well, she could just hear Max say he was leaving town "for a few days," and he'd vanish forever. Or hear him say, "Well . . . I suppose they could make it into a movie for TV . . . My set hasn't worked in six years."

Just thinking about it was bad enough.

She telephoned Sonia.

Sonia, her godmother, was the ex–movie star who long ago had arranged the meeting between Mort Leven and Harry Katz. Sonia now lived in New York. The last time Jacaranda had heard from her was on a postcard from Venice (Italy), which said, "*You* belong in Italy, my darling." But now, according to Mae, Sonia was home and Jacaranda dialed her New York number for the first time, though Sonia's old Hollywood number was still in her memory—even Sonia's *old* old number, when the prefix was CRestview and there were only four numerical digits.

"'Ah-looooo," Sonia answered.

"Hi!" Jacaranda cried.

"Leven!" Sonia said. "Ahhh, Jackie, how are *you?*"

"*Fine!*" Jacaranda said; she couldn't wipe the smile off her face now for all the tea in China. "How was Venice?"

"Very beautiful, but the tourists—" she said, and asked, "When can you come?"

"I'm leaving on Sunday . . . It's, what, Monday now—right?"

"Sunday in the morning or at night?" Sonia asked.

"Night."

"Come Sunday, in the afternoon, I will put the other off. Goodbye, goodbye, the lawyers are here now. I have to get them coffee," Sonia said. "Goodbye."

Jacaranda put down the phone. Whenever she talked to Sonia, she always thought she smelled flowers.

eve babitz

Tea for Three

Wallace wanted to ride his bike over to the Russian Tea Room but Jacaranda wouldn't let him. "You want me to take a cab *alone*," she cried, "and you ride your *bike?*"

"Oh, O.K.," he said gloomily.

"Your manners are so rotten I'm learning from your mistakes," Jacaranda said in the cab. But the air was filled with merriment, the cabdriver wasn't angry. The city was so madly beautiful and nobody could do anything but go along with it—the worst month (except for August) had turned into a springtime romance. It was not muggy, not gray, not hot, not like a steam bath; it was *spring.* "It's probably got something to do with the bomb," was all the cabdriver could hurl into their minds, "but it sure is gorgeous. Ain't it?"

"Gorgeous!" Jarcanda promptly agreed. "A great day to ride your bike."

Wallace Moss slid her one of his looks on an icy platter.

The Russian Tea Room was too much for her. It looked like a rehearsal for "The Flight of the Bumble Bee" done in crimson satin buzzes, all that red, and she went straight into shock, spiraling out into the feeling that she and the Russian Tea Room were one. A kindly numbness allowed her to sit at the table talking and observing and otherwise fooling people, but in truth she was looking out through a windswept, cool glaze. Someone should have told her that after drinking the amount she'd been drinking, one could not expect to stop suddenly without blowing off a cliff and out over the Grand Canyon, so far had she to fall before she got back to earth, so high had she been. No wonder they called it euphoria. It was like being in a hang-glider in the palm of fickle breezes. Only in the Russian Tea Room.

"Welcome to New York," Janet Wilton said, contained like a Victorian lady, greeting people day after day, but still virtuously cordial. When you put her voice together with how she sat, greeting Jacaranda with one out-stretched precise handshake, her voice suddenly did not sound like a stone but more like politeness.

All her life, Jacaranda had felt impatient with so much as lipstick, but now here was Janet Wilton, a paragon of cosmetic art, seeming perfectly all right—natural, in fact.

Jacaranda could not even eat with lip gloss on; she didn't really feel that shoes had earned their right to be counted as a member of her wardrobe, because shoes were just *shoes* all the time (and if you walked on sand, you didn't need shoes).

"Hello, Wallace," Janet Wilton said, fast enough for the Russian Tea Room. "How did it go this morning?"

"She and Lloyd Cavendish are going to get married," he said.

"Oh," Jacaranda said. "I did just love him."

Janet Wilton was the kind of woman one used to read about in books put out by modeling-school personalities, the people who said that it didn't matter what you actually wore just so long as you were self-possessed and emanated stylish nonchalance. These books were always telling girls to "be yourself," and if that doesn't work, then try having a vivacious personality or being a good listener or joining a school club. But Janet Wilton would always be the one who didn't mind wearing a party dress to a cookout, the one who turned it all into an asset, the belle of the ball, forever.

No matter what was in fashion, Janet Wilton was a step beyond. She was the one everybody was trying to become, except that the minute they became Janet Wilton, a curly brunette with blueberry mascara and rapist-slash cheek toner, Janet had turned into a French blonde with a simple powdered nose, and was suddenly pink instead of pomegranate.

Jacaranda, after careful study, had decided that Janet Wilton was basically about five feet seven, had brown hair and brown eyes, and freckles on her nose. Her face, Jacaranda was fairly certain, would probably have looked perfectly nice with just rouge, but Jacaranda couldn't imagine it because she couldn't imagine Janet Wilton away from New York, from fashion, and from shopping.

Janet Wilton pillaged when she went shopping, and it was with Janet for the first time, one day in Bendel's, that Jacaranda came to realize how much shopping is like cocaine, both being expensive transient bursts of well-being.

Jacaranda began to feel that Janet would be a dear friend. Not a "dear friend" like on the barge, but a truly dear close old friend from high school, who had always been smart, and always been pretty, and was briskly moving ahead, being accurate and swashbuckling and hating sports and winning all the debates and all the prizes that smart girls win.

Jacaranda felt the warmth of Janet Wilton's tantalizing behind-the-scenes manipulation. She felt that between Wally Moss and Janet, where she sat right then, she was perfectly safe. And if she could only get Shelby in with her, she'd be safe and happy.

"What will you have to drink?" the waitress asked.

"Club soda with a twist," Wallace Moss said, mumbling his "please" afterward so only a stag could hear it.

"A Kir," Janet Wilton said, "please."

"Club soda with a twist, too, please," Jacaranda said, feeling it sounded elegant and that she'd solved her entire problem of what to order in bars from now on. If she could just get that sullen look of Wally's and garble her "please," she'd be perfect.

"Get the chicken," Janet told her, "it's good here."

"Oh," Jacaranda said, glad not to have to decide because the menu words wouldn't stay on the menu. "Could I have the chicken, too, please?"

They all had chicken.

"You didn't say 'please,'" Janet said. "I know how you live, Wally. You never go out! But I've got to come to this place every day."

"I said 'please!'"

"He did," Jacaranda said, "really. You just couldn't hear it very well. I heard him say it."

"Well, speak up, Wally," Janet said.

Jacaranda was shocked.

"Don't worry," Janet, in an aside, told Jacaranda. "We went to camp together. And he was, really, a royal pain."

"Oh," Jacaranda said.

"And she was always modest and even-tempered," Wallace explained evilly.

God, the *pace,* Jacaranda thought. They have the energy for this!

"Anyway"—Wallace turned back to Janet—"I'm reading the manuscript you sent over."

"I told you it would need a lot of work," Janet said. "Didn't I? Isn't that what I said when I had the three moving vans drop it at your office?"

Wally improved the design his silverware made on the tablecloth, and said, "It's not as if he was Jacaranda, where you know just by reading her that it's going to be all right."

If only she wasn't trailing away in bumblebees and red satin, she said to herself, she might have been able to concoct an attitude more suitable to the discussion of literature. But Jacaranda felt unable to resist the siren song of the Russian Tea Room's walls and desires, a song that sounded like Mussorgsky run through an elevator-music process. She tried to look deeply thoughtful, frowned into nowhere, and hoped no one would notice she was listening to "Night on Bald Mountain" played by a thousand and one strings.

"I mean it's not as though every word is your last and they all have to stay exactly the way you wrote them—but that's not what I mean either. It's just—this writer is a difficult person and you're not."

"Far out," Jacaranda said, roused practically to consciousness by such a pronouncement.

Wallace Moss looked at Jacaranda and said, "Don't say 'far out'; even if you are from California."

"I can't help it. When I'm deeply moved, I speak from my heart," Jacaranda said. That anyone should think she wasn't difficult made the whole world bloom in fresh horizons. But then it all went back to red.

"Anyway," Wallace Moss said, "I'm not really loving this manuscript, Janet."

"You guys!" Jacaranda said sighing, giddy with bliss.

"What do you mean?" Janet Wilton said.

Wallace's sexy eyes were sliding around the table. He wanted to talk about Jacaranda's book.

Jacaranda didn't stand much of a chance with the two of them there all sane and serious, so she went back under her cork tree and chewed her cud and felt the strength of their strong minds wrap around her like a sable coat in the Russian Tea Room, where nobody at all was having tea.

Paying for Lunch

"**Y**ou *paid* for the lunch!" Wally said. Janet Wilton had slipped her American Express card to the waitress in a sleight-of-hand move that Jacaranda had just caught by accident through a mirror.

"So?" Janet asked.

"This was *my* lunch!" Wally cried.

"Your lunch? So you take her next time," Janet said.

"There won't be any next time . . . You know I don't eat lunch. Besides, this was her first lunch in New York and I wanted to take her!"

"She's been in New York before," Janet said, snapping her three-hundred-dollar purse closed.

"Ohhh," Jacaranda said as it finally dawned on her. "I . . . uh . . . Listen," Jacaranda told Wally, "I hardly ate anything. It wasn't that good anyway."

"She knew it was *my* lunch," Wally grumbled as Janet left to go make sure her hair looked the way it did, in the ladies' room.

"She's faster than you," Jacaranda said. "You've got to watch her hands all the time. Why don't you take me for lunch when we can be alone?"

Jacaranda just loved Wallace Moss now, but she knew he would never *do* anything about it. She was beginning to get discouraged again and think he didn't like her, but then this little cloud, this smile, crossed his face like a young sailboat cloud, a little white meringue in the middle of that full-blooded red satin interior. "Tomorrow," he told her, "you should drop by the office."

Jacaranda smiled, again knowing that he liked her all at once. "I'll bring my lunch."

"Great!" Wallace said. "And we can talk about your next book."

Complicated Woman, Complicated Dream

Jacaranda and Janet stood on the sidewalk as the people crackled past them with intense grips on themselves to keep from leaping into the spring air. The afternoon was even more shameless than the morning.

"I can't believe this," Janet said, awestruck by the beauty, as Wallace pulled away in a cab, thank God (just the two of them!). "I can't even wear my sunglasses, it would be criminal to hide any of this."

They began walking toward Janet's office, a few crosstown blocks away, through streets that were sharp with blindingly marvelous reflections, like a dream of pirate cargo, laden with treasures, glittering and shimmering. Luckily, Jacaranda was so numb that walking through these canyons of steel—past the fountains, which were worse—was easy.

They passed treasures from everywhere on earth. Each shop was more beautiful than the last; each shop had its own shopping bag, its own purpose. Jacaranda discovered that in New York the way to tell that you're happy is by shopping—and when you actually *buy*, you're in heaven.

"Wally was so anxious to meet you," Janet said, straight off, "he called twice."

"He did?" Jacaranda said. "I wish you had told me."

"What for?" Janet asked.

"You only told me I couldn't con him. I just about died wondering what else to do," Jacaranda said.

"Yeah," Janet said, stopping at a jewelry window looking at an emerald necklace.

"What'd you tell him about *me?*" Jacaranda asked.

"You?" Janet squinted at the emeralds. Jacaranda couldn't believe someone was actually considering emeralds that big. "Nothing. Maybe I just told him he couldn't pull any crap with you because you were too smart for him."

"Oh," Jacaranda said. "*I'd* be too smart for *him?* No wonder he was afraid to meet me."

"He wasn't *afraid* to meet you," Janet said, clarifying her thought. "He was afraid you wouldn't *like* him. There's a difference."

"Oh," Jacaranda said.

They sailed into Janet's office building, which was outwardly all black glass, and sailed into open elevator doors with the coming-back-from-lunch-late people, and sailed out on the tenth floor where A.I.M. Literary Agents had their offices, as opposed to A.I.M. Movie Star

Agents, the Rock-'n'-Roll Agents, and the European Film Distribution Department.

One of the only things Jacaranda knew for sure about the agency was that Etienne didn't own it. None of his companies did, though it looked like a lot of the places he did own.

Janet waved past the receptionist, who buzzed open a little gate and let them into a brightly lit—not to say florid—corridor, lined with cubicles that faced floor-to-ceiling windows. They sailed down the corridor and into Janet's office, which *was* florid. It had so many mementos in it there was not much space for a phone. But Janet had eked out a little place for an antique Florentine desk big enough to hold two hot fudge sundaes, only instead of sundaes there was a phone, and beside the phone were pink message slips, an inch high, left during lunch. On the walls were an original Jim Dine, a Ruscha, and an enormous silver "wow." Jacaranda spotted a couch, which at first, in her condition, she thought was an Andy Warhol flower. But there it was, a whole couch, and empty. She flopped right down on it.

"How could Wallace Moss be afraid to meet me and then act like . . . I don't know." Jacaranda couldn't think. "He's so *mean!*"

"He *is* mean," Janet agreed. "But he's the best editor in the city, I'm afraid, so you're going to have to figure it out." She looked at the door and up suddenly: "Hello."

Jacaranda twisted her neck and looked up, too.

There, six feet four, was an enormous TV-commercial fading actor.

"Have the copies come yet?" he asked.

"No. I'll send them over to you by messenger," Janet said.

"Oh. O.K. Sorry to interrupt," he said, in an English accent, and left.

"Guess what he does?" Janet asked.

"TV commercials?" Jacaranda asked.

"No." Janet's eyes lit up with joy. "He's a member of the Royal Academy of Science. He's the top brain surgeon in England."

"He *is?*" Jacaranda asked.

"And he's written what will be a best-seller about counterespionage," Janet Wilton went on, leaning back in her flimsy little Florentine ice-cream chair.

"Oh," Jacaranda said.

"The paperback rights were just sold"—she began to yawn—"and now we're going to sell it to the movies . . ." She yawned wholly and stretched. "And I *will*"—she curled up like a cat from her stretch—". . . only not today."

"Oh," Jacaranda said.

Janet had begun turning over message slips with fingernails that must have cost five dollars apiece.

"I'm making appointments for you all this week," Janet said, looking up from her messages. And for just a moment, behind her powdered freckles, Jacaranda saw the eyes of a woman who was very, very clever. To Janet, New York

City was a large box of chocolates—a box with which Janet was familiar—she liked all of them; but she had to pick and choose which chocolate-covered cherry went with which writer. The plan was that Jacaranda would transverse the city, meet as many magazine editors as she possibly could, because "With you," Janet said, "who knows? Know what I mean?"

"No," Jacaranda said.

"I mean, who knows what you'll stir up, what crazy stuff," Janet explained. "People from California are so bizarre."

Janet then telephoned all conceivable editors and made appointments for Jacaranda to meet with them and gave Jacaranda their addresses, thumbnail sketches, and a push.

"This one is crazy," Janet said, about the first on the list. "He's a wonderful editor, but he spends two months a year in a hospital up north sticking himself back together. Just try not to look at his eyes . . .

"This one has a sense of humor, you'll be O.K.

"This one is a schmuck. He'll ask you out. Don't go. He's married and has four children.

"This one . . . oh . . ." Tears welled up in her eyes. "He never calls me anymore except on business. Oh, why does this always happen to *me* . . ." Jacaranda waited for the sobs to subside, which they did momentarily, and it was back to business: "He is a pretty good editor. He's intelligent and funny. You'll like him . . .

"This one . . ."

And on.

Janet Wilton, until she was twenty-eight, had been a happily married woman living in Connecticut and then her husband realized his life had no meaning, so he moved to Big Sur with his eighteen-year-old boyfriend, and she was alone. Coming to the great city of New York, the city of her birth, she got a job as a secretary at A.I.M. to a lowly literary agent on the fourth floor. She was now thirty-three and looking at emeralds, big emeralds, in windows.

Janet and Jacaranda were getting along without a hitch, and it was just as Jacaranda had suspected from the moment she decided Janet was the head of the sorority—smart and funny and a dear friend. From then on, Jacaranda would save whatever shopping she had to do until Janet arrived in L.A., because Janet was a brilliant consumer and would know exactly what to buy. There was only one way that things were going to happen when Janet was doing business and that was Janet's way.

When Etienne did business, he "negotiated" and spent long afternoons discussing minute points. Jacaranda had once supposedly been asleep during a meeting Etienne was having at the "bungalow," and she listened as Etienne, with infinite patience, let the enemy talk and talk until finally Etienne gave a fraction of an inch and the enemy, by that time too tired, agreed, signed, and went home.

Janet Wilton had pretty much the same relationship with all the writers she represented, which was that they could call her up any time of the day or night, drunk or insane, and she'd be reasonable and negotiate. She liked her authors to live in New York so they could be available when she needed them to appear in person at a meeting, but if they threatened suicide or got drunk or went insane too often, she would start to get angry.

Jacaranda wondered how anyone as clever as this Janet Wilton, with New York at her fingernail tips, had come to the Bamboo Café that night and given Jacaranda her card.

You're Actually *From* That Place?

Beginning on her second day in New York, Jacaranda had meetings with magazine editors. A few of these editors were people Jacaranda had spoken with on the phone from Los Angeles when she was writing pieces for their magazines, but most of them were unknown to her. The idea was that she was supposed to go into their offices and be so enchanting and wonderful that they'd be unable to resist her, and instantly assign her loads of work.

Her experience with magazine editors so far had led her to believe that they were people who *had* to know everything *before* it happened. Like Max, sort of. They had to be at every birth of a new trend, every debut, every next year's event, or person, or gang war. And had she been drinking and following those dark avenues leading to hangovers and bold adventure, she would probably have known what the future held as she once had.

However, she was hardly in the mood to be quick-witted or gossipy in her present unstable wispiness—her fourth day without a drink. It was simply not in her to do more than try to figure out what was going on and whom she was to meet and where it was that the receptionists nodded when they said it was "down at the end of the hall and turn right."

She would enter an office trying to remember if this was the editor Janet Wilton had told her was crazy.

Irwin Raplinger, her first unknown editor, looked up from a *Paris-Match* and glanced at his desk calendar so he could read who she was. Anyone who wears plaid shirts could not be crazy. Short sane brown hair grew out of his head and he wore normal glasses and he wasn't too tall.

"Soooo," he said, "you're—uh—how are you pronouncing that?"

"Jack-ah-*ran*-dah," she said, "Leven."

"I've got the last name," he said, "and you're *from* that place, are you?"

"Yes," she said.

"I don't think I've ever met anyone who was actually *from* L.A.," he said. "Were you really born there?"

"More or less," she said. "Where are you from?"

"No place," he said. "Albany."

He began looking for an ashtray under the papers on his desk and finally found one so he could light a cigarette and have somewhere to drop the ashes.

"Well," he said, exhaling, "what would you like to do for us?"

"Do?"

"Write," he explained. "What kind of article do you think might be right for us that you could do?"

Jacaranda began to feel as though she were about to ascend toward the ceiling. The gravity of the situation became diluted owing to heavy washes of euphoria that crashed over her head like breakers from the Philippines. She held on to her chair.

"Well," she said, ". . . what do *you* think I could do?"

"Uh, what sort of stuff do you do best?" he asked.

"Oh, things about L.A., I suppose," she said.

"How can you live out there anyway?" he asked. "A friend of mine went out there and they gave him a ticket for jaywalking. *Jaywalking!*"

"Oh, that's too bad."

"I couldn't live in a place like that, with no seasons. And I mean, the L.A. *Times—that's* a newspaper? You know when the Charles Manson thing came out, I wasn't the least bit surprised."

"I was. I thought this guy named Jay something did it. Everybody did. He had to go to South America until they got Manson before he could come home," she said.

"No kidding," he said. "What about a piece about him.

"Oh, I couldn't," she said.

"Why not—sounds like a great L.A. story," he said.

"But maybe Jay something *did* do it," Jacaranda replied. "Everyone knew he was weird enough."

She was having the hardest time keeping her eyes from floating out of her head and circling the room on wings.

"Jay what?" he asked then, pencil poised.

"Beefalos!" she cried, relieved. "I could do a piece on beefalos."

She tried to describe why he would love to have a beefalo story and how a piece about beefalos would so jazz up his magazine that he could run a picture on the cover under a headline like WILL THIS ANIMAL SAVE THE WORLD?

Beefalos, she explained, are a cross between buffalos and cattle, an actual genetic breed, able to reproduce into more beefalos—unlike mules, which go nowhere. Beefalos are wonderful because they are immune to most North American diseases, just like buffalos, and they grow to about one or two thousand pounds in eight months eating old cactus and broken fences—unlike cattle, which eat all that corn and soybeans.

Irwin Raplinger became depressed because no magazine editor even wants to think about soybeans for his magazine, much less have something with genetics involved in it.

Jacaranda went right on explaining how soybeans were precious food in China and oughtn't to be fed to steers, and that beefalo, according to people who'd eaten it, tasted the way hamburger used to taste.

"Well," he said, "write me a memo. Maybe one day something like it will come up."

"But this will save the world," she said.

"What about skateboards," he replied. "What's going on now in Southern California that's likely to turn into a trend like skateboards?"

"Thai food," she said after a pause.

"What do you think causes everyone to be so shallow out there? Think it's because you have no roots, or what?"

"You *are* from Albany," she said (to herself, fortunately) as she looked at him with less and less ability to maintain her countenance. Finally, she said, "Thank you so much for seeing me. I'll send you the memo. Thank you."

And she backed out the door, closed it, and was free.

"He's crazy," Janet Wilton said later on in her office. "I told you that yesterday."

"But he had on a plaid shirt," Jacaranda said.

"So?"

GOING UP IN the elevator for her second magazine-editor interview, Jacaranda made an enormous effort to think of something besides Thai food and beefalos to write about. The editor's name was Gina Tasco and she was a friend of Janet Wilton's. Jacaranda had done something for her already, so she knew it wouldn't be too bad.

Gina Tasco was tall, with feathery red hair and green

Irish eyes (only she was half Italian), twenty-six, and a top editor on one of New York's hottest publications.

"Hi," she said, clearing a place on a chair that Jacaranda had not noticed at first, it was so buried.

"I don't suppose you care about beefalos, do you," Jacaranda said, blurting all at once what she promised herself she wouldn't say.

"Oh, what a shame. We're running a huge spread on the poor things in the next issue. I couldn't believe it when I heard about the soybeans, could you?" she asked, her eyes flashing indignantly. "Feeding them to cattle when people are starving!"

Jacaranda was now stumped.

"We don't want you to write about farm stuff anyway," Gina said, her lip gloss in crescents on her Styrofoam coffee cup and not on her lips, which were nice and normal-looking. "We want you to write about real life. What about jealousy?"

Jacaranda felt her mouth water as though a lemon drop had just bloomed inside it. She breathed, "Jealousy?"

"Yeah," Gina said. "I've been saving it just for you."

"Oh, goody!"

Gina's phone rang. She excused herself, saying, "I gotta answer this, it's L.A. and I've been trying to get those mañana jerks for two days . . ." She turned her attention into the phone.

"Look, Dick, where is the manuscript; it was supposed to be on my desk Monday—now, where is it?" She paused. "Oh. . . ." She raised her eyes and looked around her office mess. "It's yellow, O.K. . . ." Her eyes landed on a yellow envelope. "Oh, it's here. Listen, I'm really sorry. Bye."

She looked up. "How do you people *live* out there? Every time I call this guy, he says something to me like 'I'll be working all weekend on my plane but I'll do it for you on Monday.' What does he mean?"

"I can write about jealousy?" she asked.

"Three thousand words by September 15th," Gina said. "I'll call Janet right now and tell her."

"Oh, goody."

Jacaranda went down in the elevator feeling accomplished and proud of herself for being able to handle meetings so consummately.

"She's a great editor," Janet Wilton explained.

THE THIRD MEETING that day took place in the offices of High Fashion where she felt as though she knew the people already because she'd done four pieces for them and was never put on hold. It was almost lunchtime. Jacaranda was bedraggled and a wreck.

"Ohhh," Rosamund Sauvage cooed, "darling, you look bushed. Can we get you anything?"

"A Hershey with almonds and a diet Pepsi," she said.

And while she ate and drank, she told Rosamund her

life story and admired her clothes, which were extremely simple, almost as though Rosamund had nothing to do all day but live in the country and count her blessings and not be managing editor of those blisteringly fashionable pages and pages, month after month.

Almost everything in Rosamund Sauvage's office was ivory: her rug, her desk, the art on the walls—everything. Rosamund wore a plain brown dress tied at the waist. She did nothing to herself that made her look less than forty-two years old, which was the age she was. She was from Superior, Wisconsin, but from the time she was ten, she knew she would have to get out and here she was.

On the ivory desk in an ivory pitcher was a bunch of dark red lilies with yellow stalks sticking out of the middle.

"Darling, don't feel you have to be in a meeting with me, you know. I'm just so glad to see you and I know how it is when you're an alcoholic and not drinking."

"Well," Jacaranda said, "I'm not exactly an alcoholic, I don't think."

"You mean, not yet?" Rosamund asked.

"Well . . ." she said.

"It's so lucky for you to be living in California. People don't worry so much out there."

BY HER THIRD day in New York, Jacaranda looked at herself in the Essex mirror and thought she looked ten years younger than the forty she'd looked in La Jolla. By the fourth day she looked twenty-five years old, and by the end of a week she looked what her mother, when she saw her, referred to as "your age, dear, eighteen."

JACARANDA SPENT A couple of more mornings in Dobson & Dalloway with Wallace Moss. It did her good to bask in the enthusiasm about her book in a place where people actually knew about books.

Things between herself and Wallace Moss seemed, at first, as though they might never smooth out. It was as though she'd never be able to be in a room with him and not be overcome with terrible portents of the future—her future—which was at stake and could blow away into the sands of time if Wallace Moss was watching her and saw something unforgivable, something horrid. Aside from that showdown the first day when she told him she was terrified (a cheap grab for sympathy if ever there was one), all she knew about him really was that he was a man who got on with things. Not that there wasn't something to be said for getting on with things—especially if one was going to be not drinking—but he was spooky, a man without a country sort of, a man without a chink.

But then one morning she discovered Wallace trying to insert a photograph into a frame. The photograph, in color but a little blurry, was of a golden retriever who, when this picture was shot, was four months old.

Wallace held the picture out for her to see.

"Just had him a month," Wally said. "I've been wanting a dog like this. Look at those feet. He's going to grow into a Thurber cartoon, bigger than a house and everything. Look at that face. Don't you love him?"

Just because Jacaranda and Hudnut had reached an understanding with one another didn't mean she had opened her heart to dogs wholesale.

"What's his name?" she asked politely.

"Casey."

"Who took the picture?" she asked.

"I did," Wally said. "Look at those eyes—did you ever see an expression like that? And that tail! You should get a dog."

"*Me?*" she said. "A dog? I have a cat. Cats don't bark."

"But cats don't do anything," Wally said. "You can't teach them to do things like you can dogs."

"I read in this book one time that you can usually teach a cat one thing."

"Yeah?" Wally asked. "What?"

"Not to grab food off the table if anyone's watching," she said.

Any man, Jacaranda said to herself, who names a dog Casey and then frames its blurred picture on the wall is utterly ridiculous and could not, therefore, get away with being spooky and make her blood run cold. He was a boy-and-his-dog from then on, and she began calling him Wally. She simply forgot he was a brick wall.

"Do you take your dog for walks in Central Bark?" she asked next.

"Is that supposed to be a joke?" he replied.

"WHAT DO YOU think of New York?" Wally asked one day when he took her out to lunch. Without Janet and the Russian Tea Room, with just Wally at lunch, New York somehow felt sensible.

"You mean, what do I think of New York?" she asked.

"That's what I asked," he said.

Jacaranda attempted gathering her thoughts and composing herself, but neither of those was her strong suit.

"Well," she said, "it's nice. But there's no burritos."

"That's silly," he said.

"Trucks just stop in the middle of the street and don't budge," she said. "They just *stop*."

"But do you like it here or what?" he demanded, impatiently turning his fork around upside down on the tablecloth.

"Well," she said, "someplace has to be it."

"Oh, come on," he said finally, a secret pleased look just beneath the surface of his face, "you love it here. Admit it."

"O.K.," she said. But she was awfully glad that L.A. didn't have to be New York no matter what. No burritos. *Or* taquitos.

IT WAS IN Dobson & Dalloway's downstairs magazine shop that she saw Gilbert Wood's four-color face flaring off the cover of *People* magazine. (She'd never met anyone connected with *People* and had never been disillusioned the way she'd been by other magazines. For her, *People* throbbed with a mysterious power and she believed everything it said.) There, right on the cover in yellow capitals, it said: GILBERT WOOD—STAR OVERNIGHT—TELLS HOW IT HAPPENED.

Inside they had photographs of him beside a motor-cycle and in his subleased apartment in Paris with Ming vases full of dead roses. A Corot hung over the fireplace. It must have been the apartment of a "dear friend." Gilbert, on the *People* cover, smiled ill-naturedly.

Jacaranda couldn't stand movies, so she had not seen the one in which Gilbert had turned into a star overnight. She had known in a vague way that he'd moved out of his apartment in West Hollywood with the cocoa-brown furnishings and the twisted sheets. Of course, he'd been an actor all along (it had been impossible to overlook) and he was practically six feet tall, so it was no wonder he'd become a star overnight. A new leading man. The world had been sadly pining for this midnight rambler and now, overnight, here was Gilbert.

She bought a copy of the magazine and took it back up to Dobson & Dalloway.

"Oh," Wally Moss said, "Gilbert Wood. Janet told me she saw him at a party last night. Women kill for him, supposedly."

"She *saw* him?" Jacaranda asked.

That mean smile of Gilbert's was too much for most men, including Wally, who shrugged indifferently at the whole flurry.

The *People* article said that Gilbert was making a movie in New York and in Paris. If he was in New York now, she decided, he'd be at the Plaza. She left a message for him to call her at the Essex. (Movie stars, she presumed, would naturally stay at the Plaza in New York.) The last time she'd seen Gilbert had been that horrible morning on the pier, with Max.

BETWEEN MEETINGS WITH editors, Jacaranda would try to stay out of the weather. She walked into shops where things on sale cost $300 instead of $420 and the saleswomen were the most gorgeous paintings she'd ever seen.

She went to Caswell-Massey and looked at the tomato gel soap and red gel toothpaste and violet scent from Parma and violet scent from France and violet scent from Devon, England.

She went to the millinery supply stores and bought a hundred dollars worth of silk flowers and three stalks of sweet peas, made in Austria before World War II, which were fading fast but she couldn't resist.

She went looking for Brandon's Memorabilia (a place one of her artist friends told her about) to load up on antique paper angels and fold-out valentines and other useless tendernesses.

She went to leotard shops, and tea- and coffee-seller shops, and museum shops, and toy shops and record shops, book shops and jewelry shops, all on one block, and decided New York was a shopping mall, pure and simple.

Every time she came to a corner with a newsstand on it, Gilbert Wood was glaring out of the cover of *People*, aflame with sex and rage. But he still hadn't called her, and the next day she would see Sonia, and then fly home.

Devant Elaine's

J acaranda and Winifred had not been out at night once the whole week. They had walked with Hudnut to Fifty-second Street to a Japanese restaurant about six, eaten dinner (Wini having a glass of white wine; she was so sane), and walked home with people—New Yorkers—volunteering to tell Wini how wonderful Hudnut was.

Jacaranda didn't feel as though she were truly *in* New York with quite the same intensity as she was *in* not drinking. To travel and be in a place at all, the way she'd always thought, you had to go out every night and pick up coyotes and wake up the next morning with a dreadful hangover and someone with no name. But now she couldn't pick anyone up for love or money. She hardly even felt like going to Elaine's that Saturday night, and wouldn't have except that she had promised Janet Wilton and she would never forgive herself if she went a whole week in New York going to bed at 9 p.m.

Besides which, she had been calling Shelby every day and finally, just before she was about to give up, he answered.

"Shelby!" she said, "you're back! Where have you . . . How is everything?"

"Darling!" he said. "I tried to call you but you and Sunrise must have gone to Mexico or something . . . Anyway, we were in Caracas and I tried to call but the phones don't work if you're not a diplomat."

"Caracas?" she asked. (There was no surf in Caracas— or was there?)

"When are you coming back? I'll pick you up," he said.

And after that the men in New York looked even more domesticated than before.

When Jacaranda realized she was leaving New York the very next night, she felt suddenly tragic for a moment.

"Well, I miss my cat," Jacaranda said. "But I'll miss Hudnut."

She could see Emilio's purring face before her. Oh, Emilio! Sunrise was probably seducing him away from her. (She'd spoken with Sunrise on Janet's WAT's line, and the creature had actually found an apartment and had her carburetor fixed for twenty-five dollars. All that in a week! Now, she'd told Jacaranda, she was looking for a job.)

"Well, I will probably miss you," Wini said. "And anyway, I've always wondered what Elaine's looked like."

"You can come, even if you won't miss me," Jacaranda pointed out. "It's not required that you like me, even, to come." She burst into tears.

eve babitz

"What's the matter?" Wini asked.

Jacaranda didn't know; she wouldn't go to A.A. and pick up even a pamphlet, which would have explained it all—euphoria to tears in half a second. She was too much of a surfer to go to A.A., so she just sat there sobbing in wonderment. No team sports for her.

Wini went and took a shower.

Jacaranda was already cleanly pressed, ready to go, sobbing.

La Mer

Jacaranda wore a French-blue smock and white cotton pants she'd found in New York at a store that Janet Wilton had never heard of.

They had been in Janet's office afterward.

"You bought that cute thing on Eighth Avenue?" Janet asked, inspecting the hem with a critical frown. "What were you doing over there?"

"I was looking for a place to sit down," Jacaranda said.

"Stand up," Janet told her.

"I can't," Jacaranda said. Once atop Janet's couch, she was not about to get up ever again. Janet waited—this was not a frivolous moment.

Jacaranda stood up, drooping.

"Wear that to Elaine's," Janet said.

"I have to," Jacaranda said. "All my other pants keep

falling down and I trip over them. I'm afraid I'll get run over. This smock reminds me of that song 'La Mer'—you know, 'Somewhere beyond the sea . . . my lover stands on golden sands?'"

"It's a beyond-the-sea shade of blue," Janet said, of the smock.

"God. You know, I don't know how you can *live* here in New York, where you have to *walk* everywhere," Jacaranda said, forgetting herself shamelessly.

The beyond-the-sea-blue smock made Jacaranda's arms look frail, and although the smock was made of cotton and billowed out like everything else she had, it did not look as if she were wearing it because she was too fat; it looked chastely fashionable, innocently sophisticated. And this, ultimately, was the sexiest way for someone like Jacaranda to appear.

She was startled at how much weight she'd lost and how definite her features were; everything showed so much more clearly than it had when she'd awakened, that Morning After in La Jolla, with a bruise on either thigh. She had no bruises now and her eye whites glistened like lacquer.

Standing back from herself before she and Wini went out, Jacaranda looked like a tulip from Holland where windmills, like her soul, whirled against the sky.

Wini was wearing an actual dress, pink, and pink shoes; with her honey hair and peachy complexion, she looked like a young lady from the Midwest about to go to church on Sunday morning. All she needed was a little pink hat. By the time they hit the street, Jacaranda was euphoric again. There they were, she and Wini, in a cab, just the two of them going crosstown. Hudnut couldn't come to Elaine's because he was just a dog.

"Dat's it," the taxi driver told them, nodding toward a dim corner place with a canopy. "Elaine's."

"Dis is it," Winifred agreed, able to read the sign from across the street as the cab pulled away.

It was Saturday night and everyone in New York was out in the Hamptons. The enormous street was deserted under the starry skies.

They entered.

At first it seemed that the only person in Elaine's was Janet Wilton, but it was early and almost at once the place began to fill up.

Janet was sitting at the second table across from the bar, where she always sat even when the place was mobbed, and that particular table was worth a king's ransom.

The place smelled the same as that deserted pier where Jacaranda had once been with Max. She began thinking of Max as though he were going to open a door and say "You're *here!*" any minute. Her senses, from not drinking, were all awry and vibrant.

On the jukebox Edith Piaf burst in to *"Non, je ne regrette rien,"* and Janet stood up, her right hand outstretched to Wini, and said, "Welcome to New York."

"Oh, thank you," Wini said.

"I'm very grateful to you for giving Jacaranda such a good home. I hear the Essex is fabulous," Janet said.

"It's O.K.," Wini said. "I don't mind. She's only here a week anyway."

Janet Wilton could not tell if Wini was kidding; most people couldn't until they'd known Wini for years and until Wini was sure they were worthy of her confidence. But Janet barely hinted that she had heard anything fishy. She swept her hand over the table and said, "My friends will be here after a screening, but nearly everyone is out of town."

"They're all in the Hampshires—right?" Wini asked.

"Hamp*tons*," Janet said.

That was it for Wini. She'd tried being polite and look where it got her. She stopped talking and nearly disappeared into the wall.

Jacaranda looked around and wished that cute Baryshnikov was there, too. She'd heard so much about Elaine's and how if you didn't sit at the right table you were in Siberia, and how people who were truly horrible were made to feel secure because Elaine gave them a good table and how others were made to feel suicidal because their special polo coats and four-hundred-dollar permanents didn't get them the table they wanted. It had sounded like just the kind of place she loved since the very first moment she'd begun the social ramble, and she'd always wanted to go. Now here she was, only she could smell Max the minute she came in the door.

Jacaranda wished she was just starting out. Wise men have always said, of course, that you reap what you sow and she'd known that what she sowed were wild oats, but wise men were so lackluster and wild oats were so shimmering and golden, even now. Wise men would never go to Elaine's, and Elaine's wasn't even that wild.

She couldn't ask Janet Wilton, "Are there any stars here?" She knew she couldn't, looking around as the place became noisier and busier and the smell of alcohol thickened. They waited for the waiter to bring the mussels that Elaine promised they'd love.

"Are there any stars here?" Jacaranda asked.

"No," Janet said. "You're the most famous."

"But what about Elaine?"

"Oh, I forgot, she's more famous."

Elaine had come over to their table and spoken to Janet, been introduced to Jacaranda and Wini, and told them about the mussels for a few minutes when they first sat down, and now she was on the telephone near the bar, talking. Jacaranda did not see how this smart businesswoman who read books could be called such a vile dragon just because she knew perfectly well who some people were and why she was putting them in front. The Bamboo Café's caste system was a little more rootless but it worked on the same principle. In the Bamboo, you got a table if who you were was either incredibly beautiful and splashy and fabulous or a producer, writer, director, or—most frightening of all—casting director, and in the Bamboo, everyone knew who was in production (making a movie) just as in Elaine's everyone knew who was writing a book. For some reason, in Elaine's it was almost impossible to pull off being incredibly beautiful and splashy and fabulous. And in the Bamboo Café, even some Elaine's customer who was a well-known genius because of public relations might wish he were a little tanner. In the Bamboo Café, writing books and knowing Janet would be considered depressingly serious. (Unless, of course, one was Jacaranda and could trick up even the literary.) Restaurants like the Bamboo and Elaine's are there to tempt one from a life of domestic oats.

Elaine's would be too obvious for the barge, Jacaranda decided; all this unpretentiousness would get on Etienne's nerves—he would not stand for places where the servants didn't appear and light cigarettes the moment a lady opened her purse. He paid money to make properly sure that all the places he went to were staffed with his sort of servants. At La Scala he always took a private room and always had extra waiters. He couldn't stand waiting for anything past 9 p.m., once he'd started to play. Elaine's was for people who'd never been on the barge, Jacaranda decided. Nobody from the barge had ever mentioned Elaine's as a place they went to in New York. So it was a halfway house between the street and the barge, this unpretentious place with the wooden chairs and wooden tables and waiters who came when they wanted to and the dusty smell of an old pier. Jacaranda wondered if she'd ever be impressed again or if she was too jaded to regain her innocence. She wondered this not a moment after having asked Janet Wilton if there were any "stars" in the place. Her brain was wavery, she noticed, and not to be trusted.

"Met a friend of yours last night at this weird party I went to," Janet Wilton said. "The *people!* I couldn't stand them. None of them seemed to have any visible means of support."

"A friend?" Jacaranda knew it was coming.

"This guy says he knows you," Janet said. "His name is Max Winterbourne."

Winifred spilled her white wine. But Jacaranda had been ready for this, so she regained her composure immediately.

"So he does know you?" Janet took Wini's response as some kind of assent.

Jacaranda said, "Well, I . . ."

"I told him we were having dinner here tonight," Janet said, "but from the look on your face, I'm sorry I didn't ask you first."

"Do we have to leave now?" Winifred asked, getting her purse and looking for a shoe under the table, ready to move out.

"What did he want?" Jacaranda asked. "Did he say anything?"

"He said he used to know you and asked how you were. I told him you were a glamorous writer and I was right—you really look beautiful, kid, what are you using on your face?"

"Nothing," Jacaranda said, her face turning pale from blood drainage. "What else did he want?"

"Are we leaving?" Wini wanted to know.

"No," Jacaranda said, "he won't show up. He'd never come to a place like this. They wouldn't."

"Oh, good," Wini said, slipping her shoes off and putting her purse down. Jacaranda, of course, couldn't eat much after that—she ate one mussel.

"I don't know about people like that last night," Janet said, tossing her expensive streaked-with-silver head. "You can't figure out what they do and you don't dare ask them. Je*sus!* And caviar, they had this fresh caviar flown in from Iran or something. I mean, it was delicious but there was this woman there, Lydia Antonia? That woman who used to sleep with all those Kennedys? God, what a mess."

"Lydia, a mess?" Jacaranda asked. Last time she'd seen Lydia Antonia—outside Etienne's mansion by the pool overlooking the city, surrounded by bougainvillaea and orange blossoms—she was oiling herself up with some sort of magic potion that cost $150 for a tiny tube and smelled like condensed eternal joy. She was forty and looked twenty and was naked and was *not* a mess. Her hair came down to her waist and it wasn't a mess either. Anyone who's forty and looks twenty naked with hair down to her waist is hard to imagine becoming a mess two years later.

"She was just falling apart," Janet said. "She was taking coke and drinking vodka straight out of a bottle and accusing us all of being swine. Mascara was dripping tracks down her face.

"Of course," Janet went on, "I know today she'll have the team in to put her back together again and she'll look like she did when she came in wearing a lynx coat, my dear, that could only have come from Paris; but it's just a little much going around in a thing like that in July."

"She's got money," Jacaranda explained. "It comes in quarterly. In cash. It's not her capital, it's dividends or something where it comes from—a trust fund?"

"Yeah?" Janet said, lighting a Marlboro. Janet looked gorgeous at Elaine's, it was exactly the right light for her; you couldn't see a freckle if its life depended on it. "I heard of trust funds. But a girl's still got to have a job. What does she do, sleep all day?"

"So she looked O.K. when she came in?" Jacaranda was disappointed.

"Tired, but O.K. She looks her age. Whatever that is. Is she forty-five?"

"*Yeah!*" Jacaranda was back to being delighted again. "Forty-two."

"Anyway, I heard about this Winterbourne; they say he's married to a Rothschild and they pay him eleven thousand a month to stay out of France." Janet exhaled from her cigarette; she looked gorgeous smoking. God, Jacaranda wished she still smoked. Janet looked about thirty-three, her age, and completely alert and curious and alive. She had none of that drugged-looking ease that comes over the faces of the women on the barge who, knowing they're safe, go to sleep. Janet was not asleep and hadn't been, except when she was married and she'd let herself indulge, but Jacaranda couldn't imagine it. Janet asked, "Is that true?"

"About the Rothschild?" Jacaranda asked. "True?"

Jacaranda never did manage to find out the truth about Max. Not even an elemental one, like how he paid for food. (The one about Max being Etienne's Venezuelan Vice-President hadn't turned out to be true after all.)

"And there was this *other* man there," Janet went on. "I've seen some sick people in my day, I've been in fast company, as they call it, but I have never *ever* seen anything like the snake he hangs around with, the eyes like heliotrope pansies. Etienne something."

"Never heard of him," Jacaranda said. "Etienne Vassily."

"Aha!" Janet pounced. "What is going on?"

"I don't know," Jacaranda said.

"She doesn't," Winifred said. "Really, she's not kidding. She does not know what's going on."

"But what *is* going on?" Janet demanded. "All those people said you were their 'dear friend.'"

"That's one of their sayings," Jacaranda said.

"Max said he 'loves you dearly,'" Janet told her. "I told him you had a book coming out after he told me you were his dear friend."

Jacaranda said, "Yeah . . ."

"Maybe we better go?" Winifred asked.

"They wouldn't come in here," Jacaranda assured her. "I know them, it's not their kind of place." (Jacaranda realized that, in effect, she'd actually checked the place out to make *sure* it wasn't.) She added, "They'd just never come in here. They'd get the bottom of their shoes all dirty."

"What is going on?" Janet asked.

"Well," Jacaranda said, "I'm the black sheep of that family. It's like trying to get out of the Mafia."

"Nobody leaves the Mafia," Janet said.

EVERYONE WHO PASSED Janet Wilton's table and was allowed to sit in the right room knew Janet and said hello or sat down for a while.

"They're all so much shorter than I expected," Jacaranda said.

"How tall are they supposed to be?" Janet said, adding, "now, tell me what's really going on."

"I used to hang around with those people," Jacaranda said. "And now I don't."

"They didn't like it when she became a writer," Winifred explained.

"Oh," Janet said, "it's simple. They're afraid you're going to tell."

"Right," Jacaranda said. "But I don't know anything."

"You do so," Janet said. "But that Max Winterbourne is in love with you."

"Oh, God," Jacaranda said.

"Are you in love with him?"

"I don't know," Jacaranda said. "I'm in love with Shelby."

"She's in love with Shelby and she doesn't know," Wini assented. "She never did know about Max. It's been dragging on for years. It's ugly. For a while there, it sort of reminded me of married people."

A look of sadness crossed Janet Wilton's face. But of course, her married life wouldn't have been ugly; she wouldn't have stood for it.

"Well, Etienne—Is that his name? He said he was going to bring everyone from the party down in a large bus!" Janet said, putting out her cigarette.

"He *did!*" Jacaranda was on her feet.

"He was kidding," Janet said. "I swear."

"Don't do that kind of thing to me," Jacaranda begged. "I'm an alcoholic and I might burst into tears." She sat down.

"O.K.," Janet said. "Look, if I see this Max person, you got a message you want me to give him?"

"Yeah," Jacaranda said after a while.

"What?"

"Boo," Jacaranda said.

"Boo?" Janet laughed. "That's it, 'Boo?'"

"Yeah," Jacaranda said. "Tell him I said, 'Boo.'"

Janet liked that.

Après Elaine's

I n the taxi back to the Essex, Wini said, "He'll call. Because of that message, you fool, he'll call."

The Last Night

A t 2 a.m. the phone rang.

"You want me to—?" Wini asked.

"*I'm* not going to," Jacaranda snapped.

Wini grumbled, "Hello?"

A pause ensued.

"He says to tell you it's Gilbert and why don't you come to the Plaza for a drink because he's leaving tomorrow morning for Paris."

"Tell him O.K., O.K.," Jacaranda said.

"She says, 'O.K., O.K.,'" Wini said, and hung up.

Jacaranda and Hudnut got up and Jacaranda dressed in what she'd worn earlier, and decided to put on some rouge even if it was only Gilbert.

"Golly, I can't believe it." Wini sighed. "Gilbert Wood. What a dreamboat."

"Come if you want," Jacaranda said, glad to hear Wini impressed, if only by a movie star.

"Can I?" Wini asked, springing up from bed and into her clothes before time marched on and things changed.

"Let's go," Wini said, grabbing the keys and her purse as she wiggled into her shoes and started heading for the door. "God, he was so cute in that movie."

"Not you, Hudnut," Wini added; "you're just the dog."

To think of Wini going to all that trouble over some movie star.

The Plaza Hotel was a block from the Essex.

Wini and Jacaranda had been awed too much by New York to have much left for the Plaza, but Jacaranda knew that if she were really herself, she'd feel the Plaza was enchanted. It was, after all, the Plaza!

"This is much better than Eden," Jacaranda said.

"Shut up," Wini said, "it's two in the morning."

Jacaranda took this to mean she oughtn't to make asides about Eden to Wini when it was two in the morning.

They took the elevator to Gilbert's floor and rang the doorbell to his suite. They waited.

"You're *here!*" Max said, flinging open the door, his face lit up in clear triumph, though when he saw Wini he instantly toned it all down and said, "I didn't expect Jacaranda to bring anyone with her."

"What's he doing here?" Wini demanded, determined to ignore Max into oblivion with every fiber of her being.

"We can always hightail it on home, you know, before this situation gets any more compromising."

"Oh, you're the friend who's Irish, aren't you?" Max asked.

Wini said, "Yeah, but . . ."

"I know because the Irish are always telling the exact truth to perfect strangers," Max remarked, the clear triumph again gleaming just beneath the surface of his voice, wagging its tail madly.

Wini laughed, her imagination captured.

"Besides, you can't go," Max said, "you just got here."

He choreographed them through the door and closed it softly.

The living room was much less the Plaza—or the way Jacaranda had imagined the Plaza—than those rooms of Max's at the Sacramento that had once seemed to Jacaranda so perfect. The place was much more muted and uninteresting; no Duchamp chess players enlivened the walls. It was as though everything had given up its claim to vivid purpose in order that Max might stand out with further definition.

He beckoned, leaning slightly toward them, his body bent like a weeping-willow branch dressed in raw white silk. His voice was as slow and Southern as a mint julep is supposed to be. His eyes were still as blue as postcard skies and as impossible.

How could anyone be so beautiful? Jacaranda wondered once again.

"He's so beautiful," Wini sighed, in an aside, under her breath.

And once again Jacaranda felt the aching waves roll over her from wanting what she couldn't have. She couldn't afford Max. That much truth cost too much.

But it wasn't how expensive Max's truths were that made her want to blot out the whole thing with three quick tequilas. It was that she lusted after him, and she knew if she ever finally did somehow catch him, he'd stop being Max. He'd especially stop being Max if he showed the least hint of wanting to so much as kiss her lips. In order for him to continue being Max when she ambushed him some night after everyone else had left, she could not kiss him; a single kiss would make him crumble into dust like dry leaves. He could never brush off passion with a fastidious shrug—for passion was much too true—and he couldn't *return* a kiss, or someone would have taken him out of circulation long ago. Nevertheless she craved Max, even knowing that if she took just one sip, there'd be no more Max, only dust. No matter how many White Ladies she drank, it always came out the same. Anyone could see it wasn't fair.

Beside her, Wini had fallen onto a chair, her pink shoes and pink dress strangely beautiful in this Plaza room, which had been designed so that almost anyone would blend in.

Max now stood across the room from them, behind the bar, his long fingers plunking ice cubes into his drink. He smiled and drawled, "What are you ladies drinking?"

"Oh," Wini said, "I'll have whatever you're having."

"And you?" Max asked, a small frown of concern as he turned to Jacaranda.

"Do you have any brandy?" Jacaranda asked.

"Of course," Max said.

"No . . . soda," she said.

"Brandy and soda?" Max asked.

"Plain soda," Jacaranda said.

A triangle had started between the three of them when Wini first went under Max's spell. Wini began to feel naked (Max and Jacaranda were both so enormously conscious of her), so that she reached for the first thing she saw, an orange, and began to peel it, filling the room with the scent of orange blossoms. The whole room smelled like an orange grove.

"Got the clap, eh?" Max asked.

"Huh?" Jacaranda said.

"Well, I thought you must, not drinking—I mean, when you take antibiotics you don't drink. So you must have the clap."

"Where's Gilbert?" Jacaranda asked. "Speaking of clap."

Jacaranda panicked. Her immediate solution for getting away was to fly out the door, flee down the stairs, and tear out into the street. There she could find some taxi to take her to the airport where she'd just sit like an Indian, arms folded across her chest, until they found a plane going in her direction—Seattle, Tucson, she didn't care, just near enough home so she could walk the rest of the way.

She could not imagine a worse catastrophe than all of a sudden finding herself with Max being polite in a hotel. A restaurant could be abandoned so easily, a street could be taxied out of, even a chance encounter at some party could be escaped—it just wasn't fair that she'd blandly walked into this living room that had Max in it. Now all of a sudden she was beset by the urge to barrel out the door.

No sooner did the strength of this emotion surge through her than it was supplanted by an enormous desire to throw herself down on the beige rug and cry; this was followed quickly by a cloud of delightful euphoria that made her curious about how things were going to turn out. Things could collapse for all she cared. It wasn't her job to keep things from being boring. In fact, she could see how things were not actually that boring straggling along by themselves. Of course, with euphoria like hers, she might be tempted to distort the truth. But then, she said to herself, forget the truth.

Max, as though she'd said this aloud, looked at her quickly, his face stricken with tact.

"Oh, Gilbert wanted to change; he'll be back in a minute," Max said. "Here."

He handed Jacaranda her glass with soda and ice and sat down across from her. To his left, Wini was now engrossed in dividing the orange into sections.

Jacaranda realized that no matter where Max was sitting—what hotel, in what city—or when, he would forever feel like home. He was a tango partner whom, after an absence of forty years, she would remember perfectly, even if she was blind.

Max touched the coffee table for a moment as he turned to Wini, and Jacaranda handed him the matches. He took out and lit a cigarette, tossed the matchbook back, and murmured, "Thanks."

They're playing our song, Jacaranda thought, "The Tango from the Black Lagoon." But she kept silent.

"What?" Max asked, looking at her.

"Nothing," she said.

Max looked at her for a moment longer, as though trying to decide with a hand for gin rummy whether to go out with under ten or wait till he had gin.

"Janet something—that woman who says she's your agent?—told me you're publishing a book . . ."

"Isn't it terrific?" Wini said. "Imagine."

"What's it about?" Max asked.

Jacaranda paused for a moment to try and think but she couldn't; whatever the book was about escaped her. Everything escaped her, come to think of it.

"It's sort of a footnote on mid-twentieth-century demography," Wini crackled, faster than a speeding bullet.

Max raised his eyebrows and looked at them both. He sighed philosophically like a good sport.

Across the living room, the door opened and there— dressed in a torn lavender-and-white checked shirt with

only one button buttoned and old jeans and no shoes—
was Gilbert. The level of sin, exploding with burning
embers, went all the way up. Wini actually clasped her
hands to her bosom, an angelic pose one would never
have imagined from her. The way Gilbert's eyelids made
his eyes blur out from a back-street romance and the way
his mouth seemed cruel beyond redemption struck up
the band in celebration of folly, causing all else to pale.
His ash-green eyes, veiled by his newly dyed dark brown
movie-star lashes, poked around the room, slowing down
the march of time.

"Hey," he finally said to Jacaranda, *"qué pasó?"*

"Oh, not much," she said. "Did you meet my friend
Winifred?"

Gilbert shambled forward. By the time he'd gotten to
Wini and taken her hand, she was flat against the back of
her chair from shock. Already that night she'd been undone
by Max—she was in no shape to face Gilbert with any composure. Gilbert held her hand too long, looking into her
eyes as he did so. Wini could hardly breathe by this time.

Gilbert sat down upon the couch next to Jacaranda,
crowding her thigh with his, and crowding her just gener-
ally against the couch's arm. He let his face fall onto her
fresh and naked neck, his lips against her ear. He smelled
like champagne.

"You smell so good," he said. "What are you doing?" he
asked. "Come with me—I'm going to Paris."

He shoved aside the hair on the back of her neck and bit her.

"Oh, I can just see you two in Paris," Max said. "To Paris, L.A. is the Center of the Universe as it is, but you two—!"

Jacaranda looked at Wini in her pink with the orange peel before her on the coffee table, and at Gilbert in his rumpled, torn, and faded old things, and at Max, a crisp white stalk of wheat with a blond straight lock that kept falling across his forehead. And herself, newly rescued from the jaws of bloated disrepair, with her nice white pants, her bluebell smock, her upside-down tulip hair, and her luminous skin. It had gotten so that her eyes were making instant little private asides concerning distance and angles and speed. They were surfer eyes and couldn't help making judgments on balance. She could imagine herself surfing through this bland beige room; she knew exactly how to do it should the furniture turn into breaking waves. Gilbert leaned into her, pulled by moons of his own, and whispered, "Stay."

Max stood up and looked at his watch, looked at the door from which Gilbert had come, and sighed impatiently. He bent down over a bowl of hotel fruit, picked out three oranges, and casually began to juggle them, holding Jacaranda and Wini spellbound until the door opened and, sleek as a sacred lizard, Etienne emerged.

He seemed to be putting the finishing touches on his cuff links and appeared to have expected the living room to be empty. He acted charmingly surprised to find anyone there.

"Oh . . . Good evening." He nodded formally.

He took possession of them with a small shake of his cuff and strode forward, an attitude of simple interest in how wonderful they all were.

"You're still here?" he asked Max.

Max looked behind Etienne as though searching for something.

"Oh," Etienne said, "the Principessa asked to be excused. She is having a headache and went out the back way. She had a headache and also tore her dress."

Etienne seemed anxious to get on to the next subject.

"Hah! *She* tore her dress?" Gilbert said.

Etienne waited silently for further remarks regarding the present episode. Max now juggled only two oranges, but with just one hand, and looked out the window without comment.

Etienne paused a moment longer to make sure the subject was closed. There were no further objections. It was, and there weren't.

"My darling," Etienne said to Jacaranda, his eyes skidding over Gilbert's hand on her thigh and coming to light with a purple flame as they landed on Winifred. To Wini he said, "But where have we met before?"

"Monte Carlo?" Wini suggested, knowing she was licked but too classy to simply give up.

"What are you drinking?" Etienne asked, turning the room into his own as he offered to serve them.

"She's not drinking anything," Max said about Jacaranda.

"You're not?" Gilbert asked. He pulled himself together and sat up straight, his hand now a mere formality on her thigh. "It's not something that can be transmitted orally, is it?"

"Perhaps she is simply allergic to alcohol," Etienne suggested. He returned to Wini, "But you're having something, aren't you?"

"Well, I asked Max to give me what he was having, only I think it's gin," Wini said. "Anyway, something's the matter with it, so it must be gin."

"But, darling, come see what you like," Etienne said, taking Wini's hand and leading her to the bar, his tongue nearly tasting her peach cheek, like the snake he was with reluctant new blondes.

Jacaranda looked at Max, who tossed a single orange from hand to hand, his postcard-blue eyes staring straight out into nothing. The clear triumph over her arrival that had been ticking inside him was now reduced to stifled yawns and one orange.

It reminded Jacaranda of the way her grandmother had always sighed, unable to hide the depth of her disappointments at the way life had cheated her of her natural place and forced her to live among those who could never understand and would wallow content in ordinariness. When her grandmother sighed, it inspired bleak gloom in all who heard. The more you tried to liven things up, the blacker and stickier you got.

Etienne drew up to where Jacaranda sat, his arm through Wini's and his eyes like purple coals.

"My darling, how good it is to see you," Etienne said smoothly now that he had a drink, "and how kind of you to bring your charming friend. Is she from the Coast, too?"

"Tarzana," Wini said.

(Sometimes Jacaranda thought the only reason Wini moved to Tarzana was so she could say she lived there.)

"Oh, well, you must . . . uh . . . *show* us Tarzana next time we're in L.A.," Etienne said perfectly. "I'm sure you know some exciting things we might enjoy. Something the tourists never get to see."

Wini burst out laughing.

Etienne looked at his watch.

"Ahhh, can we go back now?" Etienne asked Max. "Why don't we *all* go? We've been to a party and we promised to be back in half an hour . . ."

"Whose party?" Jacaranda asked.

"Mine," Etienne said. "Just a few friends in for drinks."

"But it's the dead of night," Jacaranda said. "What are you doing at Gilbert's here anyway?"

"He said he wanted to go back to the Plaza and call you before he left for Paris this morning," Etienne said. "And Max said why didn't we all go to the Plaza and call you. I said why didn't we call you from the Pierre instead, but Gilbert said he couldn't hear anything at my place because it was too noisy, and I said to use the library phone but Gilbert said he was *tired*."

Gilbert nodded, having nothing to add.

Etienne looked when he said the word "tired" as though it were an unfortunate word, one he'd rather not be forced to pronounce.

"My car is downstairs," Etienne said. "Who is coming with me and Winifred?"

"But I . . ." Wini said.

"Darling," Etienne said to Wini, his eyes scorchingly hot, "you *must* come."

"But . . ."

"If you don't like the party, perhaps you'd like to go somewhere else . . . someplace quiet. I know," he said, now gripping her elbow so she'd never get free, "Haiti!"

"Haiti!" Wini said, beginning to glow.

"A girl from Tarzana must be used to diverse amusements," Etienne said.

"O.K.," Wini said, "let's go."

Max was still standing there and didn't look as if he could move at all. But he was ready to leave.

"I'll send the car back for you," Etienne said to them all but Wini. He wanted her alone.

Now on his way out he kissed Jacaranda and made her feel at home on the barge again. He stepped back and said: "It's been *so* dreary not seeing you. Everyone is so tiresome. It isn't the same. But now here you are. Please come by and have a drink tonight if you like, darling—some dear friends, you know, nothing fancy. A very simple evening."

"Ohhh, Etienne," Jacaranda said. A horrible thought crossed her mind that Etienne might die one day and then where would any of them be.

"Yeah," Gilbert said, "just a few friends—all nine hundred of them."

"You still want me to stay?" Jacaranda asked Gilbert, curious to find out. Max and Wini and Etienne were leaving, and she might as well go down with them even though she was not going to a party at Etienne's.

"Oh, yes, please stay," Gilbert replied.

It was over quickly. Wini and Etienne walked out.

Max waved goodbye, saying, "That's why I always hate to leave—because I know you're going to talk about me."

And then he was gone and the door closed, but the room was still trembling with unrequited love.

They waited for a moment then as they sat with the coffee table between them. It occurred to her to tell Gilbert that she was only drinking soda water not because she was on antibiotics or had the clap but because she didn't want to die.

"Want a beer?" Gilbert asked. "Oh, right, you're not . . . He paused and then went on: "I can't believe any of this, you know, the Plaza . . . that *People* cover . . . this star-overnight routine . . . I mean, I knew it was all balderdash. Even when I was taking acting lessons from Colman, I knew it was . . . But I must have felt somewhere that being a star would make things like they used to be at the Sacramento— remember those parties? I thought if I got successful that it would be like that. I thought Max's parties were what success was, a preview. But finally I figured out that Max is never going to pull that stuff off again. You know, I think the reason he got so terrible in the end was because it was all his production. On your left you get the time before Max came as a margin, in the middle is the Max part—the beautiful masterpiece—and on your right is the other margin and the end of the art. Which is how you can tell . . ."

"Tell what?" Jacaranda asked.

"That it was art. That it was *his* art," Gilbert said.

Jacaranda curled her bare feet up sideways on the couch. "People who hang around Max sure talk funny."

"Yeah," Gilbert said, blowing smoke rings, "or else people who talk funny all hang around Max."

Gilbert shot her a Sacramento glance, a glance he kept in his repertoire long after Max had abandoned it. Jacaranda herself even shot glances like that around sometimes when she saw something funny and couldn't laugh except silently, in a blameless glance to someone across the room.

"Anyway," Gilbert said, "Max isn't doing it anymore, and I have the horrible feeling that if I want it like that again, I'm going to have to do it myself."

"Gilbert, it'll never be like that again," she said.

Gilbert slid to his feet and became tall and elegant; his hands became long and his voice softened to a drawl as he said to her, "Secrets are lies that you tell to your friends."

"Gilbert," she said, "you're just not slinky enough to be Max."

But she envied him. That he could even slightly be Max seemed a good thing to have handy.

Someone besides her had noticed that there was something from those days, and from Max, which still glowed in the dark, an historical incident of some kind.

The Last Dawn

They were waiting for room service to come. Gilbert was all packed, on his way to Paris to shoot a new movie. Jacaranda looked out the window where it was becoming light; no outlines were blurred in the distance the way they are in L.A., softened and yellowed by the morning dew and sunshine.

"The real trouble," Gilbert said, still talking about Max, "was that even though for him it was art, for me it was love. That's dangerous."

"But you like to go out surfing in hurricanes," Jacaranda said, "so you're used to it."

"Come on, Jacaranda," he said.

There was a knock.

The door opened and in came a waiter wheeling a room-service cart. The waiter, who was a middle-aged Cuban, said, "Mr. Wood, I wonder if you'd mind autographing this for my daughter. Just say, 'To Esmeralda' . . ."

Gilbert was handed a copy of *People* with himself on the cover and a ballpoint pen. He signed.

"Thank you," the waiter said, and left.

Looking in the mirror after a night of cocaine and opium, Jacaranda saw reflected a girl so fresh and dewy that she reminded herself of a newly uncurled leaf, only in a wrinkled blue smock. It was hard to believe New York could be so healthful after the things everyone said about it. She saw Gilbert standing beside her (looking equally fresh but nowhere near as innocent) and she smiled.

"Are those your real teeth?" he asked.

"Oh, I'm so glad I don't have to be around actors anymore," Jacaranda said, thinking of Shelby and turning to the breakfast cart.

For breakfast they had coffee and hot fudge sundaes with nuts and unsweetened whipped cream.

They both had iron constitutions.

Outside, New York had begun its Sunday best.

Wini's Wild Oat

"Oh, I'm in love," Wini sighed, returning from the Park, where she'd walked Hudnut, still in the pink dress she'd worn to Etienne's.

"Uh-huh," Jacaranda said, trying to calculate how much money she owed Wini.

"He's so *un*-rock-'n'-roll," Wini went on, looking soulfully into Hudnut's face.

"Here," Jacaranda said, handing her a check.

"Only he can't take me to Haiti because they eat dogs there," Wini said, putting the check on the coffee table where Hudnut's tail quickly brushed it off. "So maybe we'll go dune-buggying in Death Valley instead."

"Did Etienne go with you to Central Park?"

"No, he had to make a long distance call," Wini said.

"I guess my whole thing about Max was just me," Jacaranda said.

"Ohhh," Wini replied. "Well, a lot of it must have been you, but not the whole thing. Could it?"

"I think I'll save it to wonder about when I'm old and can't have fun anymore," Jacaranda said.

"Good thinking," Wini said, picking the check off the floor and putting it into her purse. "You leaving, huh?"

"Right after I see Sonia," Jacaranda said, but she had to sit down for a few minutes and be shaken by mysterious tears.

It was all gone. She knew she'd never be able to see Dobson & Dalloway for the first time, she'd never get scared of Wally Moss and hide in the ladies' room putting on lip gloss, she'd never be able to not go someplace because Max was there . . . And she'd never ever see New York in this euphoric condition. And she and Wini would probably never have dinner on Fifty-second Street in that Japanese restaurant for as long as they lived. The first time was all gone.

The Godmother

Jacaranda would leave from Sonia's to go to the airport, so she brought her baggage, the carry-on bag.

She had burst into tears again, in the lobby of the Essex after kissing Wini goodbye, over Hudnut.

Outside, it was gorgeous.

Sonia lived in an apartment house right off Central Park that had been a town house in Henry James's time and was now (since it was noisier then from horses and trams) totally solid and quiet.

The façade was respectable and subdued and there were only four floors. At one time it had been for one family. Now it was divided into four apartments, and Jacaranda, for the first time since she came to New York, could hear herself think. Even the elevator and the elevator man were quiet. (The elevator men in New York were on strike, but not in a building like this.) Jacaranda had never visited Sonia in New York; she'd only known her when she was living in

Beverly Hills in a house that was covered with flowers. She couldn't imagine Sonia living in New York without flowers, so she brought a dozen pink roses, with Queen Anne's lace, those little white speckled things, interspersed. She found out later from her mother that to celebrate Jacaranda's birth, Sonia had brought the exact same combination. "Little pink roses and those white little flowers," Mae Leven said, "just like you brought . . . when she came to see you when you were born."

Sonia, in a single moment and without so much as shedding one fake tear, had suddenly, at the age of eighty-four, decided to move to New York. She was now ninety.

Jacaranda always remembered the photograph that Sonia kept of herself, the photograph of when she was about fifty and just at the height of being a movie star. She was standing with an ocean-liner deckful of people, her hip thrust out, a foot-long cigarette holder in one hand, face smiling out with a look of seamless bliss, her hair blowing in the wind, about to take off from San Pedro to Jamaica. All the fabulous people had come to say good-bye, European-looking beret-type Hollywood people—it must have been around 1934 or so, and already the fabulous people were escaping from Berlin. Josef von Sternberg was aboard and Dietrich had her arm around Sonia. Sonia was more gorgeous; she was taller and fuller. She was as tall as Sunrise, five feet ten, and she had an oval, perfect face. Aldous Huxley and Kurt Weill and Lotte Lenya and

Max Reinhardt were all squinting in the sun, but Sonia was smiling a straight-out smile that just knocked anything in its path over, with good intentions, and then picked it up and kissed it if it cried. She had a square neckline and pearls, Jacaranda remembered, and she was holding an enormous bouquet in her arms.

Sonia's lover was a director from the silents who had made a million dollars and turned it into more millions before there were even taxes, and by that time it was in Swiss francs. He had stood only five feet four. He, too, was a Russian Jew but, unlike Sonia, he didn't stay one; he became a dapper Englishman in Hollywood and played polo for as long as he could. They were both married to other people when they started out, and were so discreet that they never rocked the Hollywood boat enough to be discovered. When her husband died, and his wife did too they went on as if nothing had happened, seeing each other every afternoon as before, sublimely enraptured with each other, divinely happy. He died quickly of a stroke, and naturally Sonia couldn't go to the funeral, since his brother's children would find out all about her (she was so discreet). She waited till the funeral was over and she sold her house on Palm Drive and went to New York. But as soon as the will had been read, the brother's children found out about everything. He had set up trust funds for the nephews and nieces in Swiss francs, but the rest was Sonia's.

Jacaranda had not been with Sonia in six years.

The last time she'd seen Sonia, in her villa blooming with birds of paradise and geraniums in Beverly Hills, he had just died and Sonia simply glowed away, only stronger, so strongly that Jacaranda had a feeling that Sonia's blood— which was probably made of pink roses—was, each evening at twilight, bled into the sunset so that she could live forever.

The thick old elevator arrived at the top floor—the fourth—and opened into Sonia's apartment. She had the entire floor. No one was there and the elevator man retired back down, so Jacaranda was alone and for the first moment in a whole week she realized there was complete and total silence. Not one sound. Paradise.

The apartment—the room she'd issued forth into—was enormous, as large as two usual living rooms, and the floors were gleaming solid wood waxed within an inch of their life. Little museum-piece throw rugs had been spaced here and there in the emptier—probably dining area—part of the living room, but over toward the windows facing the Park stood the cozy furniture she remembered from Los Angeles: the chartreuse (no, more cream-of-celery-soup) velvet luscious couch, the Marie Antoinette footstools, the remarkable chairs that were *all* comfortable and some even flowered. Paintings by Sonia's friends crowded the walls— Picassos, Chagalls—the usual old friends. (Two of the best Joseph Cornells ever created were atop the mantelpiece, two little boxes about rose thorns and dreams and houses once inhabited by princesses.) And a large Matisse.

From some distant hallway Jacaranda heard the quick tapping of heels upon wood; trying not to slip on the floor, Jacaranda stepped toward the middle of the room just as a burst of Sonia and flowers filled the air, laughter ballooned against the ceiling, silver high-heeled slippers skipped carelessly across the waxed treachery, and that voice— that deep, passionate, sophisticated, life-emboldened voice. Sonia's high heels clicked across the twenty feet of polished wood, and suddenly Jacaranda was almost fainting with the flesh, the scent, the enormous-eyed insistence; she *insisted*—Jacaranda remembered now—she insisted, "You *must* tell me everything! You must sit down beside me here, let me see you, tell me everything! But first I get the tea—or coffee . . . Sylvia is off today, I told her to go outside into the sunshine; days like these unfortunately do not often occur in this city and Sylvia is from the country, you know, from Georgia—*her* Georgia, not *your* Georgia —and she longs for her southern climate. For a week, since this sky has come to us, I have been eating nothing but sandwiches and making my own bed. She is an old woman, Sylvia, almost sixty-five, and who knows how many summers she will enjoy like this one?"

Sonia led Jacaranda (who was wearing flat shoes and who was trying not to fall down) into the kitchen, held up a carton of Lipton's tea bags with a questioning face, and said, "Only the English object to tea bags. We are Americans, we shall never notice the difference." She arranged teacups, saucers, cream and sugar (and saccharin), and spoons. Sonia forgot the napkins (like the weaver of a Navajo rug, Sonia always made sure to be imperfect lest she catch a god's eye) and—not allowing Jacaranda to take the tray for her—they returned to the living room, to the cream-of-celery velvet couch. She placed the tray on a Byzantine mosaic coffee table, and Jacaranda had just sunk onto the velvet when Sonia leaned over her, dropping petals of intensity, and demanded, "Now, tell me *everything!* How are you?"

"Oh," Jacaranda said, "for you . . ." She handed Sonia the roses.

Sonia took the pink roses delicately in her hands, smelled their fragrance (they were the only ones in the store that smelled), claimed they were her favorites, and laid them in a silver bowl, too intent on learning everything to get water for them just yet (though while they were talking, she would manage to go to the kitchen and put them in water somehow, without missing a beat).

"Well," Jacaranda said, "I'm fine."

It all came back to her, the reason she had begun thinking up good stories in the first place, the reason she had trained herself to remember details, to keep track of people, to fix things in her mind; it was all so that when Sonia was there, Jacaranda could tell her everything, make her laugh, keep her eyes widely girlish for hours and hours. Sonia had been the one to find it completely, fantastically (in the Ali

Baba sense, *really* fantastic, like Sinbad) wondrous that a child was actually growing up in a city like Los Angeles— her very own godchild!

Jacaranda saw herself sitting there, twelve years old, wearing jeans and an Elvis pin, explaining to Sonia who Elvis Presley was, playing his records, watching the comprehension of the urgency of that voice (Sonia's favorite was not "Heartbreak Hotel"; it was some B-side called "My Baby Left Me.") Sonia saw the point of the Beatles with an unstinting catch of breath when Jacaranda took her to see *A Hard Day's Night.* Sonia listened with rapt silence as Jacaranda had told her about the surfers, the *pachucos,* the girls at school—what color lipstick they wore, who was the "cutest" and why, what the words were, why only squares liked Fabian, whereas real kids headed straight for Bo Didley (which she played—both—for Sonia, born in the 1880s in Kiev). Sonia had hated the Stones until she saw Mick Jagger on TV and he'd reminded her of Diaghilev, and then she hadn't trusted him one bit, though she liked him better.

One of the reasons that Sonia, with only one servant, had always been a woman who was such an Interchangeable-with-Heaven blend of moments was that watching her have a marvelous time left you with the feeling of having experienced truly great art, art that bravely faced all of life's sorrows, joys, unbroken stretches, wealths, poverties, and sicknesses with the calm certainty that in the end when all was ashes, when the cities were buried beneath millenniums, all would still smell faintly of pink roses, until the sound of Sonia's laughter would break through the dust and the skies would slip into their blue dress again. ". . . Will you have sugar? In your tea?"

"No . . . thank you," Jacaranda said, "I'm on a diet."

"*You!*" Sonia asked, and it did look a little ridiculous for Jacaranda to complain of being fat in front of Sonia, who might elbow the Sphinx over a few feet if she felt it was in her way.

Sonia said tragically, "I do not take sugar now." And lit a cigarette, a Salem. (She once heard that menthols didn't give you cancer, so although she preferred unfiltered Gauloises, she changed brands.)

"But," she said after dropping a saccharin tablet into her tea, "tell me everything!"

So Jacaranda, knowing how Sonia liked things, began with the juicy hot stuff (the part Sonia called "risky" and *meant* risky, not "risqué," as Jacaranda, at the age of fourteen, had had the temerity to suppose aloud). She told of her book. (Sonia knew the publishers from the twenties when they were "such shy young men; one would just sit there, behind the geraniums, and pet kittens all afternoon. But he had superb taste, he chose the kitten I wanted for myself!") Jacaranda told her all about her life in Santa Monica as it was—blurry—and changed the subject to her parents and her sister. Sonia, usually unsatisfied until all blurs were explained in detail, must have sensed that Jacaranda was in a trembling state, for she did not pursue her into the present. She skipped over "everything" with one dainty sandal step.

"You have so many flowers," Jacaranda said when Sonia brought back the vase of roses from the kitchen.

"He used to bring me flowers every day," Sonia said. "Mimosa, violets, lilacs, tulips . . . Every day that we were together, every day."

She placed the roses, her back to Jacaranda, on an end table, and Jacaranda imagined she saw, only for a moment, a shadow across Sonia's shoulders, but when Sonia turned she was smiling, her eyes glittering with wicked tales of her own.

"Sonia, you're ninety, right?"

"I *will* be," she said, "next month."

"How do you stay so beautiful?" Jacaranda asked.

"Ahhh . . ." Sonia leaned back and frowned, thinking it over. "Well," she said at last, "I have a very good constitution, and . . ."

"Yes?"

"I have very good character," she said.

Sonia then launched in to her real news, which was that her enormous estate, should there be anything left over when she died, would go to the brother's children. The brother's children, it turned out, seeing Sonia living in a nine-room apartment and drinking hot chocolate all morning, writing her memoirs all afternoon, and inviting people to be entertained in the evening at her expense, had decided that the will didn't *mean* what it said and had hired five lawyers, who set out to prove it. Sonia had been protecting these non-relatives from her lover's indifference (they could go work at Woolworth's, for all he cared, but she interceded on their behalf and slipped them cars and money when he was in a good mood) for fifty years. And suddenly she discovered that they wished she was dead. She hired four lawyers herself and sold a Cézanne. ("I had seen it enough," she explained, "someone else ought to enjoy it. Besides, I was paid very well.") Her lawyers were willing to go to court. At some date in the distant future, the courts would decide these things. "Now," she craftily explained, "I do not use sugar in my tea because I understand that it is not good for you. I intend to outlive them all!"

Jacaranda watched as Sonia threw back her head and laughed. It pealed out like bells in stillness, it sang with sheer delight over such a legal entanglement, such an infinity of this lawyer and that lawyer, all these new words and phrases—"contestment" and "receivership" and "party of the first part"—it pumped freshly picked roses into her blood, it colored her cheeks, it brought an almost bluish whiteness to her eyes, her hand holding her teacup was steady as a rock. His brother's children, fools that they were, had given her immortality. They'd introduced her to a charming new subject—the law. She flourished as she listened, as the lawyers, who realized she was enjoying this, introduced her to their wives and children. (She wanted to know everything, not just about the law; she wanted to know their children's names, how their sister in Toronto was, everything.)

IT WAS SIX o'clock when Jacaranda realized that she was actually late and would have to hurry. She drew close and inhaled Sonia, the perfume of Paris and delight.

"Darling, you are leaving?" Sonia asked, with lakes of disappointed tears intimated by her frown of sadness.

"Oh, Sonia, it's been just . . ." Jacaranda looked around the room with its flowers and its elegance and its worldly humanity.

The woman in the silver sandals embraced her god-daughter, wrapping her white silk arms around the younger woman. Sonia smiled from the newness of it.

"You tell your mother how much I think of her and miss her and your father and your sister and the others if I have forgotten. You tell them I am fine and I will come and see them soon . . . But you know, Leven . . ."

Sonia's voice hushed into a secret between just them.

"I love it here in New York, it is the only city for me. Except Paris. And Venice, of course. But sometimes I miss very much California, I miss those sunsets—you know the ones I mean—but most of all what I miss from California is something one finds nowhere else on earth . . ."

"Taquitos?"

Sonia laughed; her laughter rolled around them like soft pearls.

"Well, that, too," she said. "But what I really miss is the sea. Are you still by the sea?"

"It's out my window," Jacaranda said. "It's only three blocks from me."

"Ahhh, very good," Sonia said. "I remember how I feel the first time I see you there—jealous. So beautiful it was. You go still?"

"Tomorrow," Jacaranda said, standing now by the threshold about to go home. "Tomorrow morning."

"I'll give everyone your love," Jacaranda said, one last pink-rose-kiss adieu.

JACARANDA STEPPED OUT of the elevator and into the noise of the city.

Getting a taxi to go to the airport was not easy for her, because she did not believe in taxis and did not believe— as most people did in New York—that if you waited long enough, sooner or later there'd be a taxi.

Her driver was a Latin who didn't care too much about speaking English and who drove the cab like a pinball whacker.

She tried very hard not to think, Nobody knows how to drive in New York, since it was an unworthy cliché and she kept reminding herself that it was probably because the

eve babitz

streets were just so awful that it only looked as if no one could drive in New York. After all, the parkway through Queens just wasn't the Santa Monica Freeway.

All along, since just before she'd come to New York, she'd promised herself that the moment she set foot on the plane back to L.A., she'd order three brandies and get herself back to normal. But after the tea at Sonia's and New York in general, she was afraid she'd miss something if she wasn't careful. She'd missed so much already.

And if she wasn't taking matters into her own hands by missing them, she had been busy improving them—the other of her two main tricks to liven up the landscape when it became too bland or peopled solely with boring carnivores. It wasn't that New York hadn't sometimes seemed hopeless, for it had, and yet the longer she went without improving things or missing them, the longer she would go without waking up in the middle of The End of Everything remembering Sunrise, with her cricket knees, howling on the tile bathroom floor. Sunrise bleeding in her white dress waited just behind Jacaranda's next drink. Her next drink would always be waiting for her, languishing away.

Out the window now on her right, looking back, she saw it all standing there, glistening Manhattan with its rectangular profile. Sticking out of its sides were hooks into the water to hold gigantic oceangoing vessels and keep freighters in place.

Jacaranda wished the cabdriver would go faster.

"You're lucky," her driver said, nosing into a place right in front of American Airlines. "We make great time."

But Jacaranda had always been lucky.

SHELBY WOULD BE at the airport to pick her up when she landed, a coyote with bronze eyes, waiting to take her home. Home. Emilio would be framed in a patch of sunlight, contemplating butterflies among the wildflowers tumbling down the hill. Out her window would be the ocean, a flat horizon edged in sand. In New York they could not quite believe that she—that anyone—was actually *from* L.A. She had gone to the Colosseum in the moonlight, been aboard the barge—only she hadn't caught Roman fever or been eaten by crocodiles.

Of course she'd been practicing the art of balance since she was twelve and got her first board. That may have had something to do with it. But it would never be the same. Even *she* wasn't *that* lucky.

Jacaranda's friend the casting director, whose life was cluttered with young ladies eager for a good time in his bed, had a reputation for corniness unsurpassed even by Little Nell. But there was one idea he insisted on whenever his opinion was voiced of how a movie about two lovers ought to end.

"Let's make it a happy ending," he'd propose. "In the end they'll both go their separate ways."

Jacaranda at first used to roll her eyes and say, "But,

darling, you're the only person on earth who thinks that that is how things between men and women could end happily."

"Well, it doesn't have to be forever," he'd suggest. "Maybe they could meet somewhere else in a couple—four—years, Tokyo."

But Jacaranda would just sigh. Surely an ending where they go their separate ways was grounds for tragedy even in Madagascar. And besides, when a story ended, audiences wanted a fixed place—a forever—seduced and abandoned or happily ever after, not off into the night juggling oranges, leaving the Plaza behind, going separate ways until perhaps they met again sometime in Capri or Kingston or the Hana airport in Maui, not the way she and Max had seemed to end. Every time between Max and Jacaranda was different, but it was always a tango, and the tango is not a dance that lends itself to much beyond sex and rage. The tango is an embrace popular among sowers of wild oats who regret nothing.

Tomorrow she'd be out straddling her old foam board at dawn. Only she and hardened zealots would be surfing that early. Waves that might have appeared the same to those who had never surfed would swell up and pass by. Then, as though by some commonly understood alert, the few in the water would position themselves deftly, putting their boards in the way of one particular swell, which, from afar, would seem not different to most people from the twenty or so before. But this wave would be different, it would shoot them a glance from across the waters. It would grow larger and larger, sucking in its cheeks, and, unable to contain itself, finally it would break, thundering with a passion so ruthless that nothing in its way prevailed. To ride such a stampede you had to be alive with balance, for the speed welled up beneath your feet, blooming faster and faster, as the green glass smashed into foam, throwing you into its tangoed embrace forever and ever. If you lasted and kept on your feet, the wave unrolled and unrolled until finally it exhausted itself, spent upon the wet shore, softly uncurled like a baby's smile. All waves are the same, pulled by the moon, spent at the end. But no two are alike even more.

MOST OF JACARANDA'S surf bumps had worn away by now, though she still had some scars where the surf bumps had been. She'd skinned her knees and the tops of her feet so often with those old balsa boards that her tan was always marred with jagged splotches. But on the evening she boarded American Airlines' clumsy huge jet that would thrust itself with oxen obedience into the skies and leave her down on her own white sands, Jacaranda could hardly tell where most of those scars once were. Of course she had always been lucky. As she fastened her seat belt and wished the plane would take off, she saw that all but a few scars had faded.

She had seen the very worst of the Old World seductions and had even drunk its bad waters, which were supposed to be fatal to innocent virgins, but here she still was. She'd lived to tell the tale.

About the Author

EVE BABITZ is the author of several books of fiction, including *Eve's Hollywood; Slow Days, Fast Company: The World, The Flesh, and L.A.;* and *Black Swans: Stories.* Her nonfiction works include *Fiorucci, The Book* and *Two by Two: Tango, Two-Step, and the L.A. Night.* She has written for publications including *Ms.* and *Esquire,* and in the late 1960s she designed album covers for the Byrds, Buffalo Springfield, and Linda Ronstadt.